Sinking into Darkness

A Leighton Jones Novel

*Note: the events of this novel take place ten years before those of Toys in the Dust.*

*For my big sister- who told me to keep writing…*

Copyright © 2023 N.M. Brown

The right of N.M. Brown to be identified as the Author of the Work has been asserted by him in accordance Copyright, Designs and Patents Act 1988.
First published in 2019 by N M B Books
Apart from any use permitted under UK copyright law, this publication may only be reproduced, stored, or transmitted, in any form, or by any means, with prior permission in writing of the publisher or, in the case of reprographic production, in accordance with the terms of licences issued by the Copyright Licensing Agency.
All characters in this publication are fictitious and any resemblance to real persons, living or dead, is purely coincidental.

## Prologue

1987

On the night Kelly was murdered, a rainstorm blew in from the ocean, drenching the sidewalks and tapping on the dark windows of the city, as if trying to warn the sleeping inhabitants that one of their own was a killer.

After the various libraries and sports facilities had finally closed for the night, the University of San Diego transformed from a sea of students into a sprawling and silent void. By that time those few undergraduates who lived off campus had taken the last rumbling bus into the city, whilst the remainder who lived in the residences had drifted back to their rooms before 11pm- after which only the night entrances remained open.

It was almost midnight when Kelly Coombs drove her puttering yellow Fiat along the tree-lined Torero Way, and then pulled the car into the parking lot of the Alcala Vista Residence Halls.

Beneath the bright sodium lights there sat an assortment of random vehicles- mostly older station wagons, which had often been eagerly gifted to students by concerned parents. The various colours and shapes of the cars seemed to clash with the graceful white architecture of the surrounding campus. In this particular area, neat lawns were fringed by tall palm trees, and Greek style columns formed long covered walkways which connected the grand buildings.

During the day, these areas of the campus bustled with students as they scurried to and from lectures. They would gather beneath the warm sun in animated groups, chatting and reading textbooks which were spread upon the manicured grass. However, as the university began sinking into darkness the pale stone buildings of the university became less temporary homes to several hundred young residents and more like ornate mausoleums.

After grabbing her red scarf from the cluttered back-seat, Kelly got out of the vehicle. Despite the late hour, the air outside was still reasonably war, and she was comfortable in her cut-off jeans and a grey University of San Diego T-shirt. The chiffon scarf which she quickly swirled around her neck was deliberate nod to her current fascination with California's hippy past. Whilst her many of her fellow students seemed keen to embrace the power ballads and fluorescent fashions of the eighties, Kelly found inspiration in sound and style of the Mamas and Papas. She had a pink one too but she had lost it.

Once she had locked the car, Kelly quickly left the silent parking lot and then approached the tall accommodation building. She hurried through a curved archway and walked up the stone steps, which led to the glass doors of the reception. Luckily, she had just reached the top step as the first of many raindrops began to splatter noisily on the concrete around her. For a moment, the young woman turned around and smiled at the sudden deluge.

She liked the sound of the rain hissing as it sank among the blades of parched grass. For a couple of moments, she watched as the falling rain evoked a mist which obscured the cars behind a veil of moisture.  Then, turning back to the warm glow of the building, Kelly pushed through the heavy glass door.

'Hey Suzanne,' she smiled as she entered and approached the warden's desk. 'Looks like I just beat the rainstorm, huh?'

The tall female warden sitting at reception was a student in the same year as Kelly, who had opted to take a work credit as a warden to help pay her way through college.  Kelly had undertaken a similar role in the college swimming pool. Although this meant dragging her butt out of bed every other morning, it also meant that Kelly's work was always out the way by 10 am each day. And, unlike Suzanne's job, Kelly's did not require that she speak to many people.

As was the case most nights when Suzanne was on the reception desk, the melodic sounds of The Cure was emanating from a silvers ghetto blaster located on a shelf behind her.

'Hi Kelly,' Suzanne said with a frown, 'Yeah, the forecaster on the radio said there's going to be one hell of a storm coming out of nowhere tonight. I wasn't convinced, but looks like the old guy's prediction was right. Hey, you're running a little late aren't you? You're usually in before ten.'

'Yeah,' Kelly stifled a yawn as she approached the desk. 'I was babysitting in a house over on the heights. The shift ran on a little later than I expected.'

'Up the heights, huh?' Suzanne raised her eyebrows. 'Very nice. I guess that would be a big fancy place, huh?'

'Not too fancy,' Kelly said with a small shrug of her shoulders, 'I was just helping out one of the lecturers.'

'Anyone I know?' Suzanne looked down at her notes as if only half interested, but Cara knew that the warden was most likely fishing for gossip.

'I doubt it.' Kelly shrugged nonchalantly, 'he's in humanities.'

Realising that she would be wasting her time pursuing the matter further, Suzanne glanced at the clock on the wall. 'Well, at least you made it back before the witching hour.'

'Sure did. Kelly glanced at a flurry of open books spread along the wooden reception desk.

'I take it you're cramming for next week's tests? Can't be easy at this time of night.'

'Yeah, I know, right.' Suzanne sighed. I've got an assignment Macbeth due for Friday. The assessments seem never ending, especially compared to last year.'

'Don't I know it – I should've appreciated all that free time when I had it.' Kelly lazily rubbed one of her eyes. 'Listen Suzy, I'm dead on my feet. If you don't mind, I'll leave you to hit the books and I'll hit the hay.'

'No problem, honey – you go and get some rest.' Suzanne smiled and reached for a discarded marker, then she suddenly held up her hand like someone attempting to stop traffic.

'Hey, hang on, Kelly. I almost forgot – somebody dropped off a note for you earlier.'

'They did? That's weird.' Kelly frowned. Other than a Happy Thanksgiving card featuring a cartoon turkey dressed in pilgrim attire from the Historical Society, nobody had ever left anything for her at reception.

'Sure, I was going to give it to your room-mate if she was passing, but I didn't see her tonight. Hold on – it'll be here somewhere.'

Suzanne pushed her worn chair back from the desk and began to rummage around the mound of papers and books. After a moment, she proudly produced a neatly sealed envelope with

Kelly's name printed on the front. Handing it across to her, Suzanne winked at Kelly, 'So maybe you've got a secret admirer?'

'If I do, its news to me,' Kelly said with a nervous laugh. 'Did you see who dropped it off?'

'Nope, sorry,' Suzanne shook her head. 'One of the smoke alarms up on floor three was acting up about an hour ago. Freaked me out a little when I heard it screaming away, but I went to check it out. Turned out it was just a dead battery. Anyhow, when I was on my way back I discovered that the upper level fire door had been left open.'

'Wow, why would someone do that?'

'Smoker probably – since we band smoking in the rooms here I've found a tonne of crushed butts on the fire-escape,' Suzanne said with a shrug.

'That's a little ironic,' Kelly laughed.

'Isn't it just? So, it took an age to get the door to stay closed and then by the time I got back down here, the envelope was just sitting on the desk. I guess whoever left must have waited around and then eventually got bored.'

'Very weird.' Kelly peered at the envelope in her hands.

'Yeah, I guess. Anyhow, I'm gonna need a coffee to help me cope with another twenty pages.' Suzanne stood up and turned to the back office. 'You sure you don't want one?'

'I'm good, thanks,' Kelly said as she tore open the paper envelope.

Suzanne shrugged and wandered through a small doorway into the neat back office, where she switched on the metallic kettle. If she was going to make any progress with her essay, she would probably need more than one coffee to help get her through the wee hours. She opened the small refrigerator and then brought out a carton of milk with a photograph of a missing woman printed on one side of it. Suzanne paid no attention to the carton;

she was more fixated on a couple of Coke cans at the back of the fridge.

'Hey, I've got some soda back here if you prefer?' she called out to Kelly. When she got no answer, Suzanne made her coffee and returned, mug in hand, to the reception desk.

It was then, as she sat down with a swirl of steam rising in front of her face, that Suzanne noticed the torn envelope lying on the desk. She picked it up and frowned. Glancing towards the glass entrance, she noticed that the open door was gradually closing, as if somebody had recently used it.

'Bye then,' she muttered, and shook her head in disapproval. It seemed like a hell of a night to go back outside, but Suzanne figure that if that was what Kelly wanted to do, it would be her funeral.

Suzanne, scrunched up the remains of the envelope and tossed it the paper ball into a wire basket located beneath her desk. She then took a sip from her cup, winced and then returned her attention to her course work. Whilst she slowly descended into to the realm of weird sisters and dark deeds., Suzanne was oblivious to the face that she had forgotten to put the milk carton back in the fridge. It sat behind her on the worktop like a squat white memorial to the young woman whose image it bore. Some descriptive details of her appearance were printed in a serious looking font beneath the woman's image, but this information wasn't necessary. Although the photograph was black and white, it was easy to see that the woman was in her twenties with straight blonde hair and a cluster of freckles on the bridge of her nose. In the photograph, the girl was laughing and glancing to the side of the photographer, as if looking at some goofy event or giggling friend.

After a moment or two, Suzanne – who had only circled a couple of phrases of Lady Macbeth's soliloquy- took a second sip of her coffee and decided it could do with some sugar. She pushed her chair back and stood up. It was only then, as she turned to see the milk carton that Suzanne noticed just how remarkably similar the girl on the carton looked to the student who had just left moments earlier.

'Wow,' she muttered. After walking slowly into the office area, she picked up the carton and peered at it. The resemblance was not too strong close up but it was still definitely there. Suzanne placed the carton back in the fridge, making a mental note to tell Kelly about it. She figured she'd get a kick out of it.

At the same time as Suzanne was sipping her sweetened coffee and highlighting quotations in her textbook, Kelly's unsettled mind was whirling as she drove along the dark and empty highway. She tried to focus on the outside world, but the relentless rain pouring down on the wind-shield was more than the frantic wipers could cope with. Their constant waving motion only served to blur the view of the outside world into a smeared arc of lights and colours.

The note had been confusing, but also exciting too. For the past two weeks, she had imagined this scenario over and over again – and here it was happening as she had hoped.

Eventually, Kelly pulled her car up into the rough area of land at the rear of the Oceanside Beach. In the darkness, she could see the dark outline of the lagoon up ahead. The various properties around its edge, sparkled on the dark glassy surface of the water. It looked almost luxurious beneath the cover of darkness – like a secret little oasis. Turning off the engine, Kelly sighed. At least the rain had finally stopped. If this lifeless location was where he wanted to meet, she wasn't going to argue. The place was ringed by beach homes but they were so far back that nobody would see the two lovers.

Stepping out into the night air for the second time that evening, Kelly was pleased to discover that the rainstorm had not reached this far west yet, and the sand dusting her ankles was dry.

Kelly, adjusted the red scarf around her neck, then reached into her shorts pocket and pulled out a lipstick. She twisted the end then slid a smear of cherry colour across her lips. She had only just puckered her mouth into kiss, when she heard the voice come from over her shoulder.

'Hey Kelly, thank God you came!'

Kelly turned and her eyes widened in horror.

# 1

The rain storm of the previous evening had burned itself out, leaving the sky above the Californian coast clear. This meant that at 8.30 am, the bright morning sun was already glinting off the range of glossy vehicles parked in the parking lot located at the rear of Oceanside Police Station. The place was bustling with activity as police officers, fresh for the morning briefing streamed from the shade of the single storey building to prepare their cars and motorcycles for the day ahead. It was the start of watch for several units, so various officers could be seen preparing their vehicles for hours spent monitoring the busy roads and highways.

'Morning, Officer Mead. You need a hand there?' Leighton Jones called as he crossed the hot sunlit lot to where his partner- Alice- was loading bright orange road cones into the back of their black and white cruiser.

At twenty-nine years of age, Leighton was in in good physical shape, but he didn't really expect that the smaller officer – who was in her mid-fifties-would take him up on the offer. Alice was made of tougher stuff. Plus, as Alice would often state, she had been doing the job for so long that it was generally easier to do things herself than to watch somebody else screw it up. And even though, Leighton had already been working Traffic for four years, before he was partnered with Alice, she still thought of him as being fresh from the academy.

By the time Leighton reached he vehicle, Alice had already stacked the road cones into nested piles of six and was proceeding to arrange them snugly in the trunk of the car.

'Hey Rookie, 'she grinned, 'are you suggesting that I can't manage? I'm not quite retired yet you know.'

'Not for another seven days,' Leighton winked, 'but still, maybe you should be taking it easy, winding down slowly. When my time comes, I plan to slip comfortably into a lazy retirement and you should too.'

'Piss off! You know I've never taken it easy in my life,' Alice said and continued loading the cruiser. 'I skipped the roll call this morning – damn chain came off my bike – second time this week. Did the captain give you a heads up on where we're heading today?'

'Yeah,' he wants us up on Vista Way to keep an eye on things.' Leighton shrugged. 'After the crashes last week, I don't blame him.'

Leighton was referring to four separate incidents in which three people had died as a result of collisions on the main stretch of highway which ran like an artery through the city. The most recent fatality was that of a twenty-year-old guy who had had been driving at more than one-hundred miles per hour when he had a blow-out, lost control of the vehicle and the flimsy car slammed into and around a concrete pillar of a flyover.

Alice nodded. 'Well, he can have us sitting up there watching trucks go by all week —but it's only a short term solution.'

'How come?' Leighton asked.

Alice paused and then turned to look at Leighton. She sighed as if preparing to speak to a child. He often asked for clarification, but it was never as in the form a challenge; he just wanted to understand. Alice had only worked alongside the younger officer for a little less than eighteen months but he was one of the few colleagues in a career spanning three decades that she was likely to really miss.

'Having the cruiser by the road, only slows the crazy drivers down as they pass us. We are basically a temporary deterrent; once they get out of our sight, most drivers will go back to their gasoline pissing contest.'

Leighton shrugged, then smiled. 'Well I guess slowing down for a mile or two is better than not slowing down at all, isn't it?'

Alice responded with her own wry smile. 'You're an optimist, Jonesy,' she said and then patted his arm sympathetically, 'hopefully you'll learn. But you know what? In ten days' time I won't give a shit either way. I'll be sipping Martinis by some sparking pool, whilst you'll be picking up used diapers from the side of the highway.'

'Why- you planning to toss them out the window on the way back to some rundown retirement village?'

'Fuck you,' Alice said with a wide grin.

'Hell, I'm going to miss our heart to hearts,' Leighton said. He was laughing but they both knew he meant it.

'Sure you will, oh talking of which go stand next the cruiser for a minute.'

'What?'

'Quit gassin' and just do it, Rookie.'

'Yes mam,' Leighton said with a respectful nod. He then walked to the side of the cruiser and waited as Alice rummaged in the trunk for a moment.

'There we go,' she called and then appeared in front of Leighton with a large Polaroid camera in her hand.

'Aw, you gotta be kidding! You really want a photo of this ugly old face?' Leighton asked with a smile.

'One for posterity.' Alice said and held the camera to her face. She pressed the button and nodded. 'All done!'

There was an electric humming sound from the camera, and then seconds later a square of white paper slid slowly out of the front of it. Alice gripped the photograph, pulled it from the camera and then waved it around for a moment as if swatting invisible flies.

'How's it look?' Leighton asked.

'Probably a little ghostly,' she said. 'It takes a minute to appear fully.' Alice then glanced down at the paper in her hand. 'Ah, there we go. Check it out.'

She held the image up for Leighton to inspect.

'At least the car looks good!' he said with a shrug.

'It certainly does.' Alice said and returned both the camera and photograph to the trunk.

'Okay, let's get to work, partner!' Alice slammed the trunk shut and then the two traffic officers climbed into the gleaming car. Within a few moments, their cruiser had left the order of the station parking lot and joined the surging traffic on the eight bustling lanes of Oceanside Boulevard.

## 2

Even though he was in his late sixties, Carl Jennings was still relatively competitive about his only hobby – fishing from the pier. Many of the younger guys, would show up too late to cast their glinting lines in the middle of the day. It seemed to Carl that these young bucks preferred sinking into comfy chairs and sucking on bottles of beer to the serious business of catching fish. It was enough for them to head home with a bag full of empties and couple of Calico Bass in their plastic bucket. Carl, however, was made of stronger stuff than that.

Every morning he would shuffle along two miles of beach and get settled out on the pier as early as he could. With a small folding stool and flask of iced tea, he was quite content to sit right through till lunchtime. After that, the sun was often too hot and the many expensive boats out churning over the water kept the fish away from the lines. Carl therefore believed that the time between 6.30 and 7.30 am was the magic hour when the water was quiet and some of the big beasts – Yellowtails and Amberjacks- would venture closer to the shore. But, in all honesty, ever since his wife Cheryl died, Carl's morning activity wasn't just about fishing; he also liked the routine and the company.

Carl had never been much of a sleeper, but now when he woke up in the strangely half-empty bed. there was little chance of drifting back to sleep. If he remained lying there, thoughts and memories would fill his mind, and pretty soon he would become lost in a cocktail of sorrow, anxiety and regret. Sometimes, he would spend an entire day ruminating over something he did or didn't do. Lately, he had become fixated on the fact that Carla had always wanted to visit Europe. He should've taken her to see Paris, but he never did. By the time he had seriously considered it, Carla was too ill to fly. Yet that did little too alleviate the self-criticism.

So, to avoid this, Carl would deliberately will himself straight out of bed, make up a flask of tea, gather up his rods and gear, and then head out onto the beach.

The walk along the shore was a long one, but the slow breathing sound of the ocean by his side was somehow soothing, and Carl found his many worries were usually stolen away, like smoke, into the salty air.

However, this morning Carl had slept a little later than he had intended. He had never had much use for an alarm clock, and usually his body would wake up at pretty much the same time. Although, every few weeks he would oversleep by an hour or so – never longer than that. Carl figured it was his body's way of recharging the old system.

His single storey house was a small wooden structure, overlooking the Buena Vista Lagoon. This was a vast area of wetlands, set a mile or so back from the beach. The lagoon was divided into two long bodies of water-like an elongated figure of eight- which stretched back in land for a several miles. Whilst some of the homes closer to the beach were exclusively expensive and ornate, Carl's was little more than a glorified shack- small and set further back from the beach than the luxury homes. Whilst their large residents looked out on the sparkling ocean, the only view Carl had from his bedroom window was of a neighbour's yard fence. But the front porch offered a more pleasing outlook. The area it looked on to was fringed by pampas grass and reeds Being so close to the sandy dunes gave the lagoon the appearance of some desert oasis. Unfortunately, the water filling the lagoon – although clear today – was murky and often stagnant in places. In winter months it wasn't much of a problem, but in the summer months the stink coming from the area made it seem more like an open sewer than an attractive natural feature. Many people blamed the nearby businesses for pouring all sorts of waste products into the lagoon. However, it was a difficult thing to prove. In any case, the main problem was that whatever the content of the lagoon, it had nowhere to go. As a way of dealing with the issue, many local people had suggested that the land between the lagoon and the beach could be dug away allowing drainage into the ocean and therefore a constant flow rather than a large static pools. But the opponents of this plan had argued that the ocean tides would wash back into the lagoon, killing all the freshwater inhabitants and causing a new environmental disaster in the process. However, in general, Carl didn't pay much attention to the politics of the area. He only ever thought about the pollution on the rare hot days when there wasn't much wind and he had to close his kitchen windows to block out the smell of decaying matter in the lagoon.

On this particular morning, Carl had only just left his silent house and was shuffling toward the beach at around 8am when he glanced at the large pool of water. It was then he noticed the bulky shape beneath the gently rippling surface. For one crazy moment, he thought the strange apparition was an impossibly large fish – an albino whale or dolphin perhaps, which had somehow shuffled up from the beach and become stranded in this oversized puddle. His feet scuffed across the sand, as he tried to get a clearer look. When he realised that the shape was too bulky to be a fish, Carl then figured it might be an upturned row-boat, but when he finally got close enough to the water's edge, he held his hand up to his eyes to shield the, from the fierce glare of the morning sun and realised he had been wrong.

'Shit!' Carl gasped as he realised he was looking at a small pale car sitting just beneath the surface like a toy in a snow-globe. He stepped so near to the lagoon edge that the cold water washed over his sandals. Narrowing his eyes, Carl peered directly at the strange submerged vehicle. The water was clear and shallow enough to afford a magnified view into the interior of the car.

Stepping back from the water, Carl let out a deep sigh and tried to assess the situation rationally. If the past two years of grief and panic had taught him anything, it was how quickly thoughts could spin out of control. Even watching the nightly news could send Carl's mind in a whirlwind of fears about Reagan going to war with Russians, or the whole world dying of this new AIDS disease. But Carl had a strategy for calming his fearful mind – he would close his wrinkled eyes and take a couple of slow breaths. It was something that Cheryl had taught him. During those final months he had spent every hour hunched by her bedside, he had held her hand tenderly in the desperate belief that he could keep her in this world. Yet, as always Cheryl had been much wiser and calmer than her struggling husband. Her acceptance of her inevitable and impending departure imbued her with a gentle stillness. She would look at his trembling hands and tell her husband to breathe slowly and deeply. He had followed her advice and found some comfort. It was one of the many gifts she had given him.

With a more settled mind, Carl looked at the vehicle beneath the surface, sinking into darkness. There didn't appear to be anyone in the car, so Carl figured, if there wasn't any sign of a driver, the car had probably been boosted by some kids. It was most likely that once they had finished racing it like a dragster around the boulevard they pushed into the lagoon for kicks. They had probably thought that it would stay under there for weeks – months even – and so the chances of the crime ever being linked to them was slim.

That scenario appealed most to Carl, who was eager to secure a decent fishing spot. It meant there was no real urgency about his discovery, and Carl could simply call the cops when he returned from his morning fishing trip. With a small shrug of his shoulders, he turned his back on Kelly Coomb's submerged vehicle and made his way through the powdery sand towards the distant ghostly

silhouette of Oceanside Pier.

# 3

In the spacious bedroom of his large home, the college lecturer was dressed only in a pair of pale pink boxer shorts as he stood to one side of a large window, which overlooked the gravel driveway. His tanned body was toned, but as he entered his mid-forties, this physique was increasingly difficult to sustain. His job didn't require much physical movement, and he spent most afternoons sipping a coffee and at least one piece of apple pie. But he was not one for quitting- whenever he lacked the motivation to use the rowing machine in the basement of his home, the lecturer would recall how he once been teaching an elective class when one of the buttons on his shirt had popped off. An attractive student, who he had always liked, called Angelina Martez, had joked that perhaps he need to move on to a larger clothing size. A few other students in the front row had laughed; the lecturer blushed and then ended the class ten minutes earlier than planned. That humiliation had been more than enough motivation for the lecturer to begin his new, regimented life. This involved having a rowing machine and treadmill in the basement, and monitoring exactly how many calories he consumed each day. It was a challenge to retain such a high level of self-discipline, but it was worth it when he compared himself to the other larger lecturers in the faculty.

The bedroom in which he stood was decorated in muted colours – a polished wooden floor bordered with cream coloured walls. Above his head, a ceiling fan was spinning a demented whisper. In front of him was a large wall featured two louvre style – one leading to the private bathroom; the other to a deep walk-in wardrobe.

Moving slowly, the lecturer moved his head carefully to the half open wooden shutters and glanced outside. He sighed with relief when he realised, the smooth driveway was empty. His wife had left a few minutes earlier to meet a friend for lunch and a trip to the mall in Encinitas. Usually, she would be gone for a couple of hours-eventually returning jubilant with a selection of overpriced clothes and shoes- but within those initial moments after her departure, there was still a chance that she might unexpectedly return. It had happened before, on one occasion when Lena had forgotten her purse, and the lecturer had been forced to push his collection under the bed just as the front door opened.

From this concealed position, the lecturer had peered outside. He wanted to be sure that his wife's car would not be coming back. Once he was convinced that she had driven out on to the highway, the lecturer hurried to the other side of the bedroom where he opened a louvre door and then stepped into the cool shade of the walk-in wardrobe. He flicked the light switch on and then dropped slowly to his knees. To an observer, it may have initially appeared as if the college lecturer had chosen this private location in which to recite a prayer to some unknown god. But that was not the reason for his strange posture; he was simply retrieving a hidden item.

Breathing quietly, he carefully reached his right arm into the narrow space beneath a row of pressed pants. His hand scrambled around in the shadows like a fleshy spider for a few moments until eventually he found the focus of his search. His fingers made contact with the item, which had been pushed to the farthest corner. He gripped the corner of the cardboard shoebox and then pulled it from its resting place.

After carrying the shoe box from the wardrobe, he crossed the room then sat on the edge of the bed. He carefully placed the box on his knees. Even though he knew the house was empty, the man still glanced instinctively over his shoulder towards the window. He waited for a moment, listening for the groan of a car engine or the click of heels approaching the door of the house. There was no sound other than the distant hum of a lawn mower in some neighbour's garden. And so, satisfied that he was alone, the man placed his thumbs under the lip and raised the lid of the box. He then gently placed this to one side and looked into the box of secrets. A flicker of excitement rippled through his body.

The lecturer once again glanced nervously over his shoulder, as if making one final check, then he reached into the box and removed a long pink scarf. Holding it up to his face he closed his eyes and inhaled the faint ghost of some sweet perfume. A smile creased the sides of the man's mouth. For almost an hour, he repeated this action with the many different items that filled the box. He would touch them, brush them against his skin, smell them and occasionally lick them. To him, these were priceless; each of them had once belonged to a different dead girl.

## 4

At the end of a long shift on the side of the sweltering, noisy highway. Leighton felt like he needed a long, hot shower to wash the dust, sweat and exhaust fumes from his skin. He and Alice had dismantled their temporary traffic stop, like a circus packing up the big top before making the journey to the next town, and then they set off on the return journey to the station.

On this rare occasion, Alice had graciously allowed Leighton to drive the cruiser. It was standard protocol that seniority would determine who was at the wheel, this was then followed by length time in service. If both officers were of similar age and stage, a simple coin toss would suffice. Superstition and policing often went hand in hand, so no cop would ever challenge the decision of fate. If the coin said it was your turn to drive, you would accept this guidance from the hand of fate gracefully, or risk never seeing the end of watch.

'So, do you fancy heading over to the Rooster for a beer tonight?' Alice asked as they turned off the sun-baked highway on to the four lanes of the Boulevard that ran through Oceanside like a major artery.

'Nope,' Leighton said, 'I promised Heather I would stay home tonight.'

'Really,' Alice raised her eyebrows. 'I thought Mrs J would be happy to get a break from all those dinner table chats about traffic violations and misdemeanours. You know, my ex-husband used to tell me that cops should only ever marry other cops, because apparently we pretty much only ever talk about the job, and if we're not doing that we're thinking about the job.'

'Sounds about right,' Leighton said and nodded as he shifted the car over to allow an impatient van to pass.

'Frank always said it was like a club that only people on the inside understood.' She glanced down her hands for a moment rubbing absently at the place where a ring had one been. 'I guess it took all kinds of dumbness not to have seen that divorce coming,' she said with a small laugh at her own expense.

'His loss,' Leighton said with a smile.

'Damn right!' Alice said.

Leighton was about to ask Alice if she liked living alone, but he wasn't sure how to formulate the question without is sounding like some type of accusation. In any case, he never got the chance to ask it. The conversation was interrupted by a crackle as the car radio stuttered to life.

'Any units in the vicinity of Bueno Vista Lagoon. Respond.'

Alice reached forward and picked up the radio handset. 'This is Adam 322. We are in the area- heading north west on Carlsbad Boulevard. Go ahead.'

'Adam 322, we have a report of a car in the water. A local fisherman called it in.'

Alice shot Leighton a look of mild curiosity. He smiled and shook his head.

'The car's in the water?' Alice asked. 'Isn't that the coastguard's problem?' Alice sounded almost hopeful.

'Negative, Adam322. The car is not on the beach; it's in the lagoon. Repeat – the car has been reported as being in the lagoon.'

Alice glanced back at Leighton and raised her eyebrows in surprise.

'The lagoon is pretty big. You got an exact location, dispatch?' Alice asked.

'Affirmative, Adam322. Address is 3 Ocean Street.'

'Roger that. Me and the Rookie will take it. Out.'

Leighton hit a switch on the dashboard and the cruiser siren began to moan into a banshee cry echoing into the clear blue sky.

# 5

The young man sat almost perfectly still on the edge of his wooden bed in the small room in the Santa Anna halls of residence. He was smoking a Marlboro cigarette and occasionally tapping the crumbling ash into a beaded glass tumbler which was located on the floor between his feet. A red checked shirt hung loosely around the young man's thin frame like a grain sack on a scarecrow, and his dirty blonde hair was long enough that it hung around his face in greasy shards.

The room, which was the cheapest type on campus, consisted of the wrinkled bed, at the foot of which was a wooden long surface with served both as a writing desk and a dining table. Upon the desk sat a red angle poise lamp and a row of creased paperback books. His latest addition- a crisp copy of Stephen King's 'It' sat to one side. The cover of the novel showed a pair of monstrous eyes peering out from a storm drain, and the title was printed in garish ketchup red ink. A Hershy bar wrapper was peeking out from between the pages, where it provided a temporary bookmark. The young man had only started reading the novel a couple of days before, but he had tumbled into the adventure as fully as if he had fallen through a trapdoor and he was already about half way through. Being such a quick reader, the young man had fully expected to finish it within a couple of days, but that had been before he acquired something much more distracting.

The white cinder block walls around the young man had seemed cold and sterile when he first moved into the residences. However, over the course of four semesters, the walls had gradually become adorned with posters of fantasy movies – gifted by a local Blockbuster video shop. Some of them had been torn at the edges, but he had carefully repaired them with scotch tape before selecting the best location for each. His favourite two- *Lady Hawk* and *Highlander* were attached with scotch-tape to the ceiling above his bed. It was against dorm regulations to attach anything to the ceiling but he would remove them before the Spring Break room inspection. Sometimes, the young man would lie back on his bed for hours and gaze at the posters- imagining that he was transported into some mist-shrouded past where there were monsters to be defeated and sultry princesses who would fall into his welcome embrace. But today, he was not looking at his posters; today his troubled gaze was fixed upon the door opposite his bed. It was there, upon the chrome handle of this door- which led into a cramped shower room- that a red lanyard was hanging. At the bottom of the lanyard hung a laminated identification badge featuring the University of San Diego logo and the words 'pool attendant'. Beneath these words was a faded photograph of smiling, blonde girl in a white t-shirt.

The young man had looked at the image for so long that his eyes hurt. He was unsure of the exact time he had spent looking at it, but suspected it had been at least three hours. And yet he still could not look away. Whilst a twisting curl of smoke rose from his cigarette like a tormented spirit, the young man's thoughts were

spinning in a cocktail of desire and guilt... mostly guilt.

# 6

As their cruiser pulled off Ocean Street onto a sloped road- dusted with sand- which led down to the lagoon, Leighton and Alice were confronted with a waist-high yellow metal barrier. It extended across the entire road and was hinged at one side. At the side of the barrier was a printed sign, mounted on a metal post, which stated in large black print that the area was designated for resident parking only.

'Well, that's not good,' Leighton said.

'Just one more problem to solve, Rookie. Let's see what we're dealing with.

Both officers got out of the car and approached at the barrier, which was secured in place by a thick brass padlock.

'Looks like we'll be making the rest of the journey on foot.' Alice said.

'I could always take the grinder to it?' Leighton suggested.

Alice looked at him and shook her head in mock disappointment. 'I know you're eager to get your big toy out, Rookie, but it's better to know what we are looking at before we go destroying anybody's private property. We can just climb over.'

'Sure. But do you need to a hand getting over that thing?' Leighton asked with a cheeky grin on his face.

'You need a kick in the ass?' Alice replied. She then gripped the metal railing and vaulted over more easily than Leighton would moments later.

As they sauntered down the ramp to the stretch of sandy ground, which was located a quarter of mile back from the beach, Leighton and Alice were already glancing around looking for signs of a possible accident.

Whilst nearing the water, Leighton wrinkled his nose. The war air seemed sharp with the smell of ozone and seaweed, but down here in the lagoon there was darker scent that reminded him of the murkier ponds he had fished in as kid.

'Stinks a little, doesn't it?' he said as he gazed around.

'Yep,' Alice replied, 'It's from all the shit pumped into the pond. I'll bet the realtors always choose a windy day when they bring the millionaires down here to sell them a big beach house.'

Approaching the water's edge, Leighton crouched down and peered at the strange spectacle of the submerged car.

'What do you reckon,' Leighton chuckled, 'should we write it up as a 586- illegally parked?'

'Always with the funnies,' Alice said but she was smiling.

After making a brief inspection of the location of the car, Alice left Leighton by the water's edge and promptly returned to the cruiser. Sliding into the driver seat, she lifted the handset and began sharing their discovery with the dispatch team.

Whilst his partner was busy, Leighton stood up and began surveying the area for potential witnesses. There were only a couple of buildings nearby- one was a boat house; the other was a fishing supplies depot- both of the places looked like they had been shut for a long time. Further back on the other side of the lagoon there were a number of larger houses – the kind that were fringed with tall palm trees and private pools. Leighton knew that the people in these houses were unlikely to have spent the previous evening watching the stagnant lagoon, which lay beyond the tall walls of their exclusive homes.

Of course many of the exclusive beach houses were also empty – having been purchased as second or third homes. Leighton wondered for a moment what kind of job would give people enough money to buy a three-million-dollar home for use every other weekend. Most of the occupations Leighton could think of were fully or partly illegal.

He returned to the water's edge and crouched down to examine two parallel lines of shallow indentations in the soft ground. They were a few inches apart and snaked from the water for a few yards before fading into the fringe of softer sand. It was difficult to identify the nature of the imprints; the rainfall of the previous evening meant that the lines had lost whatever definition they might have had. It was impossible to tell if they were linked in some way to the sunken car or not. After standing up, Leighton took a few steps along the shore of the lagoon. He peered around trying to figure out how a stolen vehicle could have got through the locked gate.

After a moment, Alice appeared by Leighton's side again.

'You got something, Rookie?'

'Probably nothing,' Leighton said as he stood up.

'Well, I spoke to dispatch and they're sending Jon with the pick-up,' she said, 'allowing for traffic on the boulevard, I guess he should be here in a half hour maybe longer. I've moved the cruiser to give him access.'

'What about the padlock?' Leighton asked.

Alice laughed. 'Jon Cortez is used to separating cars that have been smashed together at 120mph. That little lock will be like a ring-pull on a beer can to him.'

'I get that. D' you think the winch will reach all the way in there?' Leighton nodded towards the water.

'It had better,' Alice said, 'or I guess you might be skinny dipping.'

'I've had worse duties.' Leighton said with a shrug of his shoulders.

'Yeah, but like I said there's all sort of shit in that water. I reckon further up the lagoon where it runs close to businesses that this pond will be used a convenient waste disposal. There's five or six food places back there that could easily dump their used fryer oil into the lagoon.'

'Talking of food places, I spotted a Starbucks over on the Boulevard on the way down here, you want me to take a walk over grab us some coffee and a couple of pretzels to take out?'

'Now you're talking, Rookie.' Alice said with a smile. 'I knew there was a reason why I liked you better than any of my other partners.'

'Yeah, well I guess you're easily bought,' Leighton said.

'That's what comes of my time working in Vice,' Alice said with a laugh. 'You want me to come with you - just in case you screw up the order or get robbed by some middle-grade kids?'

'Nope,' Leighton shrugged and began to walk away, 'I plan to get up there before the place closes, and you'd only slow me down.'

'Just go get the fucking coffee,' Alice said with a grin.

7

Lucy Sanders instinctively felt that something was wrong. It wasn't much of a hunch as a certainty. As she stood in the doorway of the room she shared with Kelly Coombs, Lucy could hear the muffled sound of some Blondie song margining into the steady murmur of conversation coming from one of the other rooms on the same floor, there was a faint aroma of frying vegetables and cumin emanating from one of the other apartments, but her own room was silent, cold and gloomy.

The previous day, she he had arranged a study date with Kelly as they both wandered out of the bustling lecture hall. Lucy had wanted them both to visit the library on both Monday and Tuesday, but Kelly had said that she couldn't because she had been given a last minute baby-sitting gig. When Kelly pleaded that she really needed the support, Kelly solemnly promised to invest all day Tuesday studying with her. She was a dependable friend who up until now had always kept her promises.

Lucy had first met Kelly the previous year when they were housed in the same accommodation block. Although at that time their single rooms had been at different ends of a long dark corridor, Lucy and Kelly were the only two students who regularly cooked their own food in the cramped communal kitchen. This meant they initially spent mealtimes together eating different food. Logic eventually prevailed and the pair began doubling up and sharing the cooking. It was an efficient and comfortable arrangement. So, when the opportunity to share a two-bedroom apartment in second year arose, both young women were delighted and hastily submitted a request form for a place in the Alcala Vista building. Lucy and Kelly were initially denied a place missing out on the last free room by just one day.

However, one of the other two students who had been due to take it had fallen prey to acute appendicitis. Her potential flatmate had opted to move into her boyfriend's cramped apartment rather than have to find the missing rent money each month. As the next interested parties on the list, Lucy and Kelly were offered the place and were delighted to accept it. The rent was higher than getting a place off campus, but the location had made it much easier for both of them to pick up employment. Whilst Kelly worked poolside in the college swimming facilities, Lucy worked making and serving desserts in one of the many eateries. The timing of shifts in their respective jobs meant that the girls were often home at different times so would leave small notes, food and an occasional candy bar for each other. Sometimes, to Kelly's delight, she would open the refrigerator to discover Lucy had brought them freebies from work in the form of wedges of key lime pie or strawberry cheesecake, which they would later devour whilst watching some cheesy afternoon soap on television.

When Lucy, awoke to a quiet apartment on Tuesday morning, she assumed that Kelly had come home quietly the previous evening whilst she had been asleep and then, in the morning, had left early for her shift at the pool. This would not have been unusual- Kelly was a considerate flatmate and would therefore tiptoe around wearing sneakers to avoid disturbing her friend.

Having spent all of Tuesday scribbling notes alone in the library, Lucy had eventually wandered back to the large block of residences. It would have made sense for her to expect to find Kelly at home, possibly cooking them both some pasta, or watching General Hospital – either of which she particularly enjoyed.

However, now after she opened the door to a cold and empty apartment, Lucy knew something wasn't right. She stepped inside and then slowly closed the door. There was no sound of any activity and the place felt lifeless.

'Kelly, are you around?' she called as she placed her notepad and books on their small dining table. There was, as Lucy expected, no reply.

Wandering through to Kelly's bedroom- which was adorned with posters of Richard Gere movies, Lucy discovered Kelly's pool uniform was still sitting folded on top of her drawers where she always placed it the evening before every shift.

If Kelly had gone to complete a couple of hours at the sport centre she would be wearing those clothes, and, as far as Lucy was aware, Kelly did not have two sets. This was always a source of stress, because if she had to work two mornings back-to-back,

Kelly always had to wash her stuff in the communal laundry as soon as she finished.

The fact that her uniform was still in the apartment meant that Kelly had not come home the previous night. It was this realisation that unsettled Lucy more than anything. Kelly had never stayed out all night before.

## 8

Jon Cortez, the lumbering, tattooed driver of the recovery vehicle, had spent almost an hour in the water, where he had been engaged in fastening a combination of oil-stained belts and clanking chains to the vehicle, whilst Alice and Leighton assisted by standing by the barrier, ushering curious residents away from the scene.

One of the locals – a white haired lady in expensive looking jewellery and a pink velour track suit- had tried to be helpful by telling Leighton that she had been walking her beagle – Samson- the previous evening and had noticed the barrier was up. Another elderly resident- sporting a neatly trimmed moustache-had claimed to have seen a red car down by the water, but when pushed, he had scratched their head and stated that it might have been a different car – or perhaps it had been a different evening. Leighton thanked the witnesses and took down the statements, but doubted they would be useful. Eventually, after realising that the combination of a large truck blocking their way and limited access to the lagoon meant there was no way of seeing what was happening, the locals drifted away – probably to spy on the events from their own homes.

Alice and Leighton wandered back to the scene.

Wading slowly from the water like some type of dripping swamp creature, Jon brushed his long fringe back from his face and addressed the police officers.

'Okay, I've attached the slings as best I can. Now, you need to understand that this is going to play out one of two ways,' he said with the weight of experience pressing on the words.

'What do you mean?' Leighton asked.

'Well, if the car is not in gear and the bottom of the lagoon is fairly solid – rock maybe- it should just roll right up here to meet the truck.'

'And what if it's not?' Alice asked.

Jon glanced back at the water. 'If it's sitting on a mixture of sand and mud, and the car is in park, it'll most likely dig in like a good old anchor. The more I pull, the deeper it'll bed in.'

'Then what?' Leighton asked. He could already feel the day slipping away from him.

'I guess you'd then be looking at using a crane – which'll be a fucker to get down here. But hey, I'm an optimist, we might just drag it right outta there,' Jon said and approached the rear of his truck. 'In either case, you two need to step back away. If one of these slings snap, there's a real chance you'll get hit in face with a sixty pounds of steel chain, and that will kill you quicker than a 9mm round between the eyes.

The two officers did not need to be told more than once. Both of them withdrew back to a safe distance.

Luckily, moments later, Jon discovered he had been correct when he stood by the truck and pulled the lever to start the winch. There was a churning groan then a loud clink as the chains tightened. Whilst Jon casually held on to the juddering lever, like a someone running a fairground Ferris wheel, Leighton and Alice watched as the sunken vehicle began to emerge from the lagoon.

Eventually, when the winch had slowly reeled the car out like a harpooned whale, the small crowd of onlookers had clapped weakly and then- without the excitement of seeing a dead body at the wheel- had quickly dispersed back into their harbour-side homes.

Jon switched of the winch motor and then wandered over to where Leighton and Alice stood.

'You guys need some time to sniff around the car before I tow it back to the station?' the large man asked.

'Sure,' Alice replied and looked at Leighton who nodded. 'You sure that's okay with you, Jon?'

'Suits me,' Jon said with a stretch of his thick arms. 'I'll be happy to go for a smoke and then pick up a burger from somewhere local?'

'Thanks,' Alice smiled, 'me and the rookie will be as quick as we can.'

'No rush,' Jon said as he sauntered back to his truck to collect his wallet and a pack of Marlboro cigarettes.

Having been slowly freed from its watery confinement, the dripping car was now sitting like a guilty pet at the edge of the darkening lagoon.

'What do you reckon, is it stolen?' Leighton asked as he wandered around the car.

'Unless there's somebody the trunk, I'd say that's a pretty good guess.'

'Shit!' Leighton looked suddenly haunted and stared at Alice.

Alice caught the expression on Leighton's face and realised what he was thinking. The previous summer a couple of park rangers had discovered an abandoned car in an isolated area of Guajome Regional Park. According to the rumours, the vehicle had sat there for a couple of days before they finally got round to opening it. That was when the rangers found a deceased kid in the trunk. The coroner was not able to tell if he had died before the car was dropped off. That meant there was a real possibility that the kid had still been alive in the stifling vehicle whilst the hikers and rangers were sitting at the picnic tables a few feet away from it.

It was later confirmed that the car been stolen from outside a lumber store in Corona, seventy miles north of Oceanside. The kid had been abducted the same day from a shopping mall in San

Bernardino but his killer was never caught. The case had sat like a weight upon all cops for many months, and had only recently began to fade into the collective consciousness of the police department.

Leighton walked around to the driver side of the car, pulled on his latex gloves and then opened the door. A flood of water poured out and he had to step back quickly to avoid soaking his feet.

Once the deluge had subsided, he moved back to the side of the vehicle and crouched down. He had half expected to find the ignition switch had been burst open with a couple of wires twisted together. But he was surprised to discover that a set of keys featuring a mini Rubix Cube key chain hanging in the ignition slot.

'Looks like it wasn't boosted. I got keys over here!' Leighton called to Alice.

'Nice. Could still be stolen though. Any house keys or similar attached to them?'

'Nope,' Leighton replied, 'just a mini toy.'

'Okay, just leave them in place. Jon will need them for taking off the steering lock. When he gets it back to the pound.'

'Sure,' Leighton said, but he wasn't really listening. Instead, he was looking at the wind-shield mirror. It had been twisted all the way around to face the opposite way around.'

'What's up?' Alice asked. From over his shoulder.

'Take a look at the mirror.' He got up and moved aside to let Alice lean in.

'Pretty weird,' she agreed with a small nod.

'It's not just at an angle; it's twisted right round.'

Alice peered at the rest of the interior. 'It's possible that when the car went into the lagoon the force of the water rushing in did that.'

'I guess,' Leighton shrugged, 'You want me to check the trunk?'

'Go knock yourself out.' Alice said.

Leighton walked over to where Jon was sitting on the sand having a smoke. He looked like he was enjoying the sunset.

'You got a crowbar I could use?' Leighton asked.

Jon nodded. 'Sure, there are about five of them lying next to the winch. Help yourself.'

'Thanks.'

After selecting a suitable lever, Leighton walked to the rear of the small car and slid it in the narrow gap between the lid of the trunk and the body of the car. The metal resisted for a moment then the lid sprang open like a jack in the box, but there was nothing inside it other than a yellow umbrella and a bloated collection of Shakespeare's plays. Leighton wondered how much the book had cost.

'No corpse?' Alice asked from by his side.

'No,' Leighton said, 'thankfully.'

Alice yawned and stretched her arms. 'Then I guess Jon can take this baby to the garage, I can hit the gym and you can get home to hit on your wife.

'Amen,' Leighton said and slammed the trunk of Kelly Coomb's car shut.

9

Despite Alice's instruction to Leighton, her impression of Leighton's home life was not entirely accurate. By the time Leighton Jones arrived home, the apartment was already empty. He had hoped to get back in time for dinner. That at least could have provided a moment when he and Heather would be together for a little while. This was something he had been trying to do recently, but it was harder on the weeks when he was working late shifts but at that time the rota had meant he had four weeks of day shifts.

In recent months, things hadn't been so great between him and Heather. Partly it was because of his job, and partly it was because of Heather's studies, but mostly it was simply because of life.

They had met when they were both in their final year of high school in Fontana. At the time, Leighton had a part time job in the steel works but her had already started completing his admission forms for the military. His plans, however, changed when over the course of that July he quickly became intoxicated by the cocktail of youth, and love and seemingly endless summer days Then suddenly the prospect of leaving Heather behind seemed inconceivable. They had spent countless afternoons eating picnics in Fiesta Park or hiking the trails that criss-crossed the hills. For the first time in his life, Leighton felt good about himself and the future. That was one of the main reasons he chose to work in law enforcement. Having already invested months in getting into good physical shape and with a need to have some sort of structure, joining the academy seemed almost as appealing as the military. It offered a uniform he could feel proud in and a sense of community. He and Heather got married two years later in a small service in Winchester and then settled into a few comfortable years together. In his naivety Leighton had somehow imagined that they would always spend afternoons at the beach, or tangled together in the darkness of their small bedroom. But real life was not like that and a coolness crept in to the relationship. Occasionally, Heather – who had taken a job working as a supervisor in a local delivery company- would complain that if she hadn't met Leighton she would have gone off to college and her life would have been very different.

After eight years together, it was clear that they had both changed. In recent months, most of their interaction had been either neutral or negative.

Leighton padded into the small kitchen and found a small note lying by the sink. Picking it up, he scanned the writing.

*Gone to class. There's salad in the fridge. Heather x*

Leighton smiled. At least there was a kiss.

After he had tidied the small apartment, Leighton took a long shower, then lathered his face up with foam and had a wet shave. Sometimes, during the night, he would curl his arm around his wife and touch his face against her shoulder. Heather's response was always to pull away from him in the darkness. If he commented on this, she would simply say that his face was too scratchy and rough. Leighton figured that maybe if his face was smooth and soft, Heather might not pull away.

After rinsing the sink, Leighton walked into the bedroom, switched on the temperamental air condition unit on lay on the bed. He let his body settle for a moment and then picked up his battered paperback from the night stand. It was a horror story about a possessed car. Heather had told him that it probably wasn't the best story for a traffic cop to read, but Leighton liked it anyway.

As the AC droned a slow lullaby, Leighton read until he felt his eyes begin to close. Then, despite his best effort to stay awake, he slipped into the waters of sleep.

Three hours later, Heather Jones returned home and slipped quietly into bed, where she slept on her side so far over from where Leighton lay that she was almost on the edge of the mattress. At one point in the vague hours between one and two am, Leighton had surfaced enough from the depth of sleep to roll on to his side. Realising that Heather was next to him, Leighton leaned into her, his smooth face touched her upper arm and, almost immediately, Heather moved away from him, sinking away into her own unfathomable darkness.

## 10

Ellen yawned as she pushed open the front door of the coffee shop. A small brass bell above the door clanged, and Claire – the shop manager looked up from the area of chequer board patterned floor she had been mopping. The pungent odour of disinfectant hung in the air like a ghost.

'Hey, somebody's still sleepy,' Claire said with a smile, 'but I take it you got my message?'

'Yeah, but I think I need a little caffeine boost to get going.' Ellen said as she carefully stepped across the glossy floor to the long coffee counter.

'Help yourself to a double shot,' Claire said cheerfully as she twisted the mop into the basket of a yellow plastic bucket.

After moving behind the bar area, Ellen picked up a squat espresso cup and placed it beneath the gurgling metal machine.

She pressed a black button and a stream of steaming coffee trickled into her cup.

'I only picked up your message late last night.' Ellen called over the gurgling noise of the machine. 'I was helping my cousin Abbey to paint her new apartment – her fiancé Dean ran off with his slutty tennis coach last month and Abbey had to sell up the house on Broken Hitch Road and move into a smaller place.'

'I take it the new place needed refreshing?' Claire asked with a knowing smile.

'Hell yes! We used up six pots of peach emulsion. Think I might have some splashes still on my arms. Anyway, once we were done Abbey wanted thank me with Tacos and a couple of beers. To tell you the truth, I was kinda surprised you called- I thought Sarah Levin was due to come back in this week?'

'She was,' Claire said. 'but I canned her.'

'How come?' Ellen asked as she slipped a black cotton apron over her head. She then looped the side straps around her back and then tied them in a bow in front of her stomach.

'She was a little too friendly with some of the customers if you get my meaning.'

'Yeah, I do.' Ellen took a sip from her coffee cup. She had only worked a couple of shifts alongside Sarah, but both times she had spent so much time chatting with customers that Ellen had felt like she was the only one preparing food and making drinks.

'I was working with Angela last Wednesday. I told her that I felt like I hadn't seen Sarah for a while. She said that she thought she was on holiday.'

'Well she pretty much is. After a couple of complaints from other girls, I decided to add myself to the rota work a shift alongside her.'

'I guess you wanted to see for yourself?' Ellen asked.

'Exactly. So, I worked the Monday lunch shift alongside her.'

'I take it you ended up running the coffee machine yourself?'

'Oh I certainly did. I told her I wasn't happy with her pace of work, and that she should take a couple of weeks break then come back in and tell me if she still wanted the job.'

'Hey,' Ellen looked suddenly alarmed.

'What's up?' Claire asked with a slight frown creasing her forehead.

'I just realised that you've added yourself to the rota alongside me today. Is that because you think I'm not working hard enough too?'

'No honey,' Claire laughed, 'It's the opposite-I knew you were reliable enough that I could nip away after lunch to get my nails done.'

'Jeez, that's good to know. I was getting worried. So, what you planning to say to Sarah when she turns up – if that happens.'

'Oh, I'm, sure she will turn up,' Claire said whilst rolling her eyes. 'For some reason, the deadbeats always do. So, I'll tell her to take the job seriously and stay the hell away from that smiley college professor she seems to like chatting with so much.'

## 11

There was a noise in the darkness. At first, Lena Brookes thought she had heard a low rumble of thunder – it wouldn't be that unusual. The weather over Oceanside in the previous two weeks had shifted from blue skies to lightning storms and hurricanes. However, as she became more fully awake Lena realised it was the low rumble of her husband's car crunching on the gravel. She turned her head and blinked at the glowing red numbers of the clock radio on the night stand. It was a little after midnight. That meant she had been sleeping for an hour. She had hoped he might return earlier.

Around dinner time, Steve had called to say that he had an important faculty meeting to attend and so wouldn't make it back home in time for supper. Lena had asked if she should leave him something in the pot, but he said he would grab something from the commons kitchen on his way across campus to the meeting.

There was an audible click as the front door closed. That was followed by the sound of careful footsteps moving around the house. For a moment, Lina felt a flicker of fear. What if the person moving around the house wasn't actually Steve? Some stranger might have crept into her home whilst she had stupidly felt safe. Her heart rate began to increase, until at one point she heard Steve drop his keys into the glass fruit bowl in the hallway. Lina breathed a sigh of relief. This was something her husband did every time he came home and was as recognisable as his voice.

Eventually, she heard him enter the large bathroom, then the sound of a shower running echoed along the hallway.

There was no need to use that one; they had an en-suite, and yet he did.

Fifteen minutes later, Lina was still awake as Steve slipped out of his towel in the darkness then slid into bed beside her.

'Late night?' she whispered and took Steve's hand. She brought it across and placed on her warm naked stomach. 'I've been waiting for you,' she said, 'I'm not sleepy.'

'Yeah, sorry.' he said and pulled his hand away. 'I went back to the office after the faculty meeting. Must've fallen asleep in the office. I'm just done in.' He rolled away from his wife in the darkness and then fell silent.

Lina said nothing, but for long after her husband had sunk into the warm waters of sleep, and was snoring, she lay awake in darkness so thick it was almost tangible.

Two hours earlier when her husband had got off the phone line, Lina had realised that she didn't know if she should fix dinner for Steve or not. She didn't want to pester him- which he hated- but if she knew what time the meeting was scheduled to end, she could have something ready. Lina had therefore picked up the phone again and called the main college switchboard.

It had taken a few calls before anybody answered, but the woman Lina eventually spoke to stated confidently that there were no faculty meetings until the following month. Steve, it seemed, was keeping a secret.

## 12

Leighton walked into the locker area of Oceanside Police station to find Alice Mead tying her shoe laces. She liked to cycle to work most days, and had often told Leighton that if she had to spend every working day in car, she sure as hell wasn't going to drive to work.

'Hey Rookie, how you doing this morning- had a little romantic night in last night did you?' Alice asked as she stood up.

'Yeah,' Leighton said with a small embarrassed nod, 'how are you doing?'

'Just ready for another sweet day in the Californian sunshine.'

They left the room and walked through the short corridor leading to the dispatch and then the general office area shared by Traffic, Harbour and Neighbourhood – Vice, Gangs and Homicide were located in separate area.

'Any word on the Fiat?' Leighton asked.

'Yeah, I ran the plate this morning. The paperwork is on your desk?'

By now they had arrived at the entrance to the office area, but Alice stopped outside.

'Mine?' Leighton was rarely put in charge of paperwork – other than DUIs or Vehicle inspection forms.

'Yeah, you'll need to follow it up. Apparently, I have to attend a compulsory four-day course called *preparing for retirement* at the Holiday Inn in San Diego. It seems they have to teach retiring cops how to relax.'

'I thought a bottle of rum would do that for you?'

'My feelings exactly, but the big chief has spoken.'

'So who am I partnered with when you're away?' Leighton asked.

'Nobody,' Alice said with smile, 'according to the captain apparently I'm irreplaceable, so you're flying solo for a few days. That okay with you?'

'Hell yeah,' Leighton shrugged, 'I'll enjoy the peace and quiet.'

'Sure you will. Just don't damage the cruiser- it's signed out in my name.'

'Don't worry, I'll drive cautiously like you.'

'You wish you only could,' Alice said with a laugh.

'Hey,' Leighton frowned, 'what about Friday's driver awareness class- that needs the two of us?'

'It's been rescheduled for next week.'

'Jeez, the captain must want rid of you pretty bad if he's willing to rearrange things to get you ready for retirement. Hell, they must see you as some type of liability.' Leighton said with a playful frown.

'Yeah, well I'd love to stay around and listen to your bullshit, Rookie, but I have a relaxing drive to make.'

Alice turned and walked away through the maze of cluttered desks and filing cabinets.

'Wear your seatbelt!' Leighton called after her.

Alice didn't turn around but raised one hand and directed her middle finger at Leighton who laughed.

After Alice had gone, Leighton sat at his small desk. It was almost empty with the exception of a small framed photograph of him and Heather-taken in the booth outside San Diego Zoo, back when they had been happy. A black wire tray sat alongside a yellow Silver Reed typewriter. The tray was filled with registration documents for some of the vehicles which had been impounded throughout the previous months. However, sitting on the top of the pile was a newly printed sheet.

Leighton reached across, picked up the sheet and began scanning it.

The Fiat was registered to Miss Kelly Combs of the Alcala Vista Residence Halls- U of CSD. Leighton noted the irony- the Fiat had gone from one vista to another one.

The prospect of going up to the college was not an attractive one for Leighton. He had never felt himself particularly academic or privileged. He figured that the students over there would probably be both. This was exactly the type of situation where, despite the good natured jokes, he would have appreciated the company of the unflappable Alice Mead. However, Leighton knew that if he took a drive over to the campus, he might just find Kelly Coombs alive and well – having perhaps been partying with some friends for a couple of days, and all the time blissfully unaware of the fact that her car had been stolen and dumped in the lagoon.

That, Leighton figured, would certainly be a good outcome – and a quite likely one too.

Yet, there was a gnawing feeling in his gut that told him it wasn't the real one.

# 13

Dressed in chocolate coloured trousers and a white shirt, Steve Brookes bounded into the administration area of the university and offered a toothy smile to the receptionist who was peering at the screen of a large boxy computer.

'Morning Angela,' he said.

'Hi Mr Brookes,' the receptionist nodded her head in greeting but did not look up from the screen.

Steve pulled a stack of paperwork from his pigeon hole, and left the office, walking along a wide corridor leading to the lecture hall.

Although there was plenty of space in the tiled corridor, Steve fell into step behind a female student who as wearing an orange vest top and white shorts and carrying a spiral bound notepad. The outfit allowed much of her golden skin to be seen. Although, the rest of the world was oblivious to such things, Steve knew he could sense the chemical signals coming off the female students- and on some occasions staff- like a trail of scent. In the bustling corridor, he was travelling in a slip stream so powerful Steve could almost see it emanating from the student's toned body. When was a few feet behind the oblivious young woman, the lecturer inhaled deeply through his nose, consuming the bewitching cocktail of sweet berry perfume and pheromones. The heady concoction was so strong that Brookes had stop himself from physically reaching out to touch her. However, the magical connection was suddenly broken, when the girl promptly stopped to speak to some random guy. Brookes looked up ahead, in the hope of finding further targets but there were only a couple males swapping notes on their way to class.

In the absence of any further distraction, Brookes rifled through the mail as he walked. Most of it was just university paperwork. There was however one piece which was different. This was a small white envelope fringed with neatly printed flowers. The artwork seemed strangely old fashioned.

Brookes stopped walking, and tucked the larger bundle of papers under one arm as he ripped open the envelope. Inside was one neatly folded piece of paper. The words were neatly printed:

*I know about you, and you will be caught*

After promptly crushing the paper into a ball, Steve thrust it into his pocket, and hurried to the nearest empty classroom. Opening the door and stepping inside. He covered his mouth with one hand and stifled a roar of rage. He then kicked out at a nearby wastepaper basket, sending it crashing into a wall. If whoever sent the note thought that it would somehow stop him, they were very much mistaken. Steve would rather die than stop now.

He was having way too much fun.

14

On the other side of the campus from Steve Brookes, Leighton Jones stepped through the door and into the reception of Alcala Vista student accommodation block and glanced around. The spacious area smelled of floor polish and coffee. It featured a couple of pin boards covered in ads for various sports clubs and student events.

Parallel to the entrance was a long reception desk where a young man with a pony tail and Bon Jovi T-shirt was leafing through a guitar magazine. To the side of the reception desk was games area featuring a foozball and a pool table upon which a couple of students were clacking multi-coloured balls into the pockets. Leighton nodded to them amiably as he approached the reception desk.

When he glanced up from his reading material, the young man working the desk looked a little rattled to see a cop in the reception.

'Hey, I'm Dale – I mean I'm like the desk supervisor. Can I help you?'

'I hope so,' Leighton said as he approached the desk. 'We found an abandoned car down near the beach. DMV records show that it's registered to a student who lives in this block.'

'You want me to check for you?' the young man asked.

Leighton had to suppress the urge to offer the type of sarcastic response Alice would have given. 'Sure, I'd appreciate that,' he said with a smile.

'It's cool. Just hang tight for a moment.' The young man closed over his text book, 'I just need to dig out the emergency fire record. That's the quickest way to see all current residents.'

'Take your time,' Leighton said as he glanced through a wide doorway to the side of reception. He could see couches and a couple of pool tables, where a mixed group of students were clacking balls backwards and forwards without much success.

Returning his attention to the desk, Leighton found that Dale had located the red folder and opened it to display an alphabetised list of names. 'Okay, what's the name of the student you're looking for?'

'Kelly Coombs'

'That name sounds familiar,' the young man said as he turned the page. 'I only transferred here from Cal-state last month, so I'm not quite up to speed with all the names. 'Ah, here we go- Kelly Marie Coombs – Room 112. Have you been here before?'

'No,' Leighton chuckled. If he had been gained a college degree, he probably wouldn't be laying out traffic cones for his day job.

'Not a problem. The room is on the floor above this one. The stairs leading up there are just through the doorway on the right hand side.'

Leighton thanked the warden and headed out of reception to a bright hallway where two students were already descending the stairs towards him. He stepped to the side and, once the teens had passed by, he began climbing to the first floor.

The stairs led to a long brightly lit corridor with a series of widely spaced offset doors on both sides. As he walked the length of the hallway, Leighton could hear the muted sound of conversations and the distant sound of some mellow music. Arriving at the plain wooden door marked 112, he glanced down at the notification slip in his hand. Leighton felt bad for the girl. College was tough enough without discovering that some assholes had boosted your car and dumped in under three feet of stagnant water. He just hoped the kid had been smart enough to arrange insurance.

He knocked on the door and waited. For a moment, he thought the place was possibly empty, but then he heard the sound of feet padding around.

'Hang on,' came a muffled female voice from the other side of the door. Eventually it opened and Leighton found himself looking at young woman. She was wearing grey sweatpants, a white vest and had a pair of reading glasses angled on top of her head. She took one look at Leighton and burst into tears.

'Oh, hey it's okay,' he said. 'my name is Leighton- you don't need to worry. I'm only here because we think we found your car.'

'My car?' the young woman rubbed her wet eyes in confusion. 'I don't have a car.'

'You are Kelly Coombs, right?'

The young woman shook her head. 'I'm Lucy- Kelly's room-mate.'

'Sorry,' Leighton shrugged, 'Is Kelly home, can I speak to her?'

'No. She's not around. In fact, she hasn't been around for a couple of days. To be honest, I was starting to get like majorly worried about her. When I saw your uniform, I figured she had been in some sort of accident. '

Somewhere deep inside Leighton a sense of dread was starting to form.

'Can you remember the last time you spoke to Kelly?'

'Monday. I saw her right after class and asked if she wanted to head to the library after dinner.'

'Did she show up there?' Leighton asked.

'No she has a college job but she's started babysitting recently for some spare cash, I guess. She told me that she had a shift on Monday night.'

'She tell you who she was baby-sitting for?

'No,' Lucy said as she shook her head.

'And she didn't come home that evening?' It wasn't exactly a question.

'No, at least I don't think so. I have an early morning lifeguard job at the campus kitchens it's a 6.30 start, so I had gone to bed early. I overslept and so by the time I woke up and stumbled out of here, I didn't get a chance to check and see if Kelly was in bed. I mean she could've been.'

'But you don't think so?'

'No, we had a lecture at eleven a.m. in the Shiley Theatre, I kept Kelly seat but she never showed.'

Leighton nodded. 'Can I ask if anyone else has a key for your apartment –friends perhaps?'

'Not really,' I gave my mom a spare key for safety, but she lives in Oregon and hasn't been down here since we moved in.'

'What about Kelly's folks?'

'No, she only has her grandmother and she's in a care home in Kansas City.'

'Okay Lucy,' Leighton said in a reassuring tone, 'you've been really helpful. I'll try to find out what's going on.'

'Will you let me know if you find out what's happened? I just want her to be okay.'

'Sure, I'll keep you posted. Thanks for talking to me,' Leighton said and then left.

As he was walking out of the residence's reception, Leighton was oblivious to the fact that he was being watched intently by a scrawny young man in the red checked shirt who was standing by the scuffed pool table in the general games area.

'Hey, Corey it's your turn,' another student said impatiently.

Despite hearing this statement the young man, who was holding his cue like a weapon, still didn't take his turn; he just kept watching until Leighton had slipped from his field of view.

## 15

Jared Martinez liked his job. On Thursday nights, some of the other guys at in his team down at the Surf Bowl would joke about him spending his working day waist-deep in shit. They would smirk and wrinkle their noses at him whenever he was running late and arrived in his grey work clothes, but they were too dumb to realise how lucky he actually was.

San Luis Rey Wastewater Plant facility was located four miles outside Oceanside, in small valley surrounded by gentle green hills. Although the site was a water treatment plant, the area was spacious and attractive. The various lakes around the area created a local micro climate which supplied the many plants and animals with an abundance of fresh water- a scarce resource in much of San Diego. The combination of fresh water, clean air, wildlife and lack of pollution made the location seem like a lush oasis in the middle of a desert.

The work was good too. Most of the time Jared – who had originally trained as an AC installer – was only required to monitor water pressure at various points around the plant. Occasionally he would be required to change a filter, or replace a leaky rubber pipe seal, but other than that life out there was sweet. However, better than all of these features was the fact that this job meant Jared could still regularly take a smoke break whilst at work. Whilst many of his buddies were increasingly banned from smoking in their offices and factories, Jared was free to wander away from the main buildings to have a smoke and take in the stunning views. He liked working the late shift most of all because that meant he could watch the sunset.

As well as the square treatment pool, the site was also close to Lake Whelan, which had recently been donated to the community as a wild bird sanctuary, the site was also home to the much smaller Windmill Lake and another couple of large pools.

He had been standing looking at the blue sky above the three smaller pools of water where a Kestrel was circling in the warm air like a plane waiting to land. Jared figured that the bird was observing some small prey before moving in for the kill. He'd seen it happen a couple of times before. Once, he had been out checking the seals on an overflow pipe when, a bird swooped silently out of nowhere and then lifted an oblivious lizard from behind a rock.

This time, Jared was determined not to miss the show. He followed the bird's line of sight from the sky down to the landscape, but instead of seeing any sign of a small creature scuttling across the landscape, Jared's eyes were drawn to one of the three smaller lakes. This particular one was wider than the others- a D-shaped body of water located nearest to the buildings of the water processing plant. Halfway across the small lake- just below the surface- was something that clearly did not belong there.  Whatever was floating beneath the surface of the water appeared to be square and white in colour. The rippling surface of the water created the impression that the object was fluttering like a pale flag in a green sky. It seemed quite possible to Jared that somebody – kids most likely- had tossed some road sign into the water.

Although he had reached the end of his allotted break time, Jared was interested in identifying the object, not only because getting water free from contaminants was his job, but also because investigating the situation would allow him time for another smoke.

Keeping his attention on the water, Jared reached into his shirt pocket and produced a red and white pack of cigarettes. With practised ease, he pulled out a smoke and placed it between his lips. He then scrambled down the steep grassy slope to the water's edge and peered through the greenish water at the strange object. It was then that the sunlight shifted through the water, and Jared realised in horror that the item he had been looking at was the roof of a submerged car. Jared's pupils widened, the unlit cigarette fell from his mouth, and snapped beneath Jared's foot as he scrambled up the grassy slope and raced towards the plant manager's office.

By the time he returned to the mirror-still water's edge – five minutes later, Jared was accompanied by his colleague Chad Jordanson and manager Bill Lewis.

'I told you!' Jared said excitedly, 'It's the damnedest thing – what the hell is a car doing in there?'

Bill Lewis didn't answer. It was clear from the pained expression on his face that he was trying to figure out the same thing himself. He stood with his hands on his hips, trying to convey some sense of authority over a situation that he couldn't understand. There was nothing in his training manuals about dealing with a car in the middle of the fucking lakes. After a moment of pained concentration, Bill turned to Chad.

'Okay,' he said, 'trying to apply some logic to the illogical. 'what's the largest size of portable pump we've got?'

Chad scratched the side of face. His nails made a rasping sound on his stubble. 'Well the water in there will be full of shit, so it would need to be the two big trash pumps. The can cope with pretty much anything.'

'How much can they shift?' Bill asked.

'They can handle about sixteen hundred litres per minute'

'Each?' Bill sounded hopeful.

'Yeah,' Jared answered this time. 'They can't run for more than a couple of hours without burning out. But I could set them off in tandem and see how they cope; I figure two hours might be more than long enough to drain the pond.'

'Good! Let's get them down here and we can see what the hell we're dealing with.'

Half an hour later, the air above the lake was filled with the roaring noise of two motorised pumps. The two shuddering red motors sat at the top of the slope. Each was protected by a square frame of tubular steel, and each was connected to a long snake-like hose leading into the water. The rear of the pumps featured open pipes which were spraying white plumes of misty water towards the nearby Windmill Lake. Bill had initially considered attaching a couple of output rear hoses to direct the water into the nearby pool, but luckily it was close by and the geography of the landscape would let the spray find its way into the larger body of water.

Once the equipment was in place and running, Bill Lewis had sent Jared back to his duties- checking pressure valves around the plant. He considered personally watching proceedings himself but didn't want the other employees claiming that their boss was spending his day sitting by the lakes and admiring the scenery. He therefore asked Chad to stay by the pumps and let him know when the water level was low enough to see what the hell was down there.

It was almost an hour later that Bill Lewis's day went from stressful to catastrophic. Bill was sitting in his office holding a telephone handset to his ear. Around ten minutes earlier, he had called up City Hall's Water Utilities Department, hoping to get advice about who was liable for a vehicle, when he heard the pumps suddenly fall silent. A moment later, Chad appeared in the office doorway. He was holding his hard hat in front of him like someone asking for a date.

Bill covered the mouthpiece of the telephone and whispered to Chad.

'Any luck?'

'Yeah,' Chad cast his gaze downwards and rubbed the back of his neck as he spoke, 'in a way. Look Bill, I think you better come down and check the situation out for yourself.'

'Sure,' Bill nodded, 'I'm just waiting to hear from the guys in the city.'

Bill half expected Chad – who he had always considered a hard-working and compliant guy- to nod his head in response and then walk away, but he didn't. Instead, he held Bill's gaze. 'With all due respect, boss, I think you better see this first.'

Something in Chad's grim expression was enough to convince Bill to replace the handset, get out of his chair and then follow his colleague out of the office. He felt a little jittery, as if perhaps he sensed he was about to see something that would regularly feature in his nightmares for the rest of his life.

## 16

In a narrow corridor in the windowless management area of Oceanside Police Station, Leighton knocked on the wooden door of the captain's office and waited. Every time he stood in that part of the station, he immediately felt like he was a kid back in middle school again.

'Come in!' came the command from the other side.

Leighton opened the door and walked in to find the captain standing in front of a narrow mirror. He was holding a buzzing electric shaver in one hand and tilting his head to look for stray hairs. He switched off the shaver and turned to Leighton.

'Officer Jones, what can I do for you?'

'Sorry to interrupt you Captain,' Leighton said softly, 'but can I speak to you – about a case?'

'Sure but make it quick. I have to address the Communities Drug Enforcement team in half an hour and I want to look over the recent figures.'

'Well, it's just that we pulled a car out of the lagoon yesterday, and it was registered to a student who is now missing from USD.'

'Okay, is that it?' the captain asked.

'No, I was over at the campus today – I visited her apartment, and her flatmate hasn't seen the owner of the car since Monday?'

'And what's your concern officer?' The captain turned back to his reflection and lifted his chin to examine his neck.

Leighton shrugged. 'I don't know —something about it just feels wrong.'

'Why?'

'I don't know – it just does.'

'Where is the vehicle now?'

'In the impound garage, drying out.'

'Did you find any evidence of a crime in the car?'

'No, other than it being located in the water.'

'Any drugs in the car?' the captain asked almost hopefully.

Leighton shook his head. 'Not that I'm aware of.'

'And did you find any physical evidence of a crime in the student's apartment.'

'No,' Leighton shook his head, 'I guess not. I asked her flatmate if there were any signs of a disturbance.'

'And was there?'

'No, but- '

The captain turned around fully and looked directly at the younger man. 'Then you need to understand that you've got nothing to go on, officer. I think any *feelings you have* that are not supported by evidence, really need to be pushed aside.'

Leighton nodded reluctantly but inside he knew he was on to something.

'Look, have you got a girlfriend, Jonesy?' the captain asked.

'Yeah, well I have a wife,' he said then added 'we married young.'

'A wife? Even better,' the captain grinned, 'what I suggest is that you get out of here, stop off at Walmart, pick up some flowers and a bottle of wine. Then get yourself home, and settle down with your wife- switch off for a little while. Maybe put your feet up and watch Moonlighting. Just try to leave the work at the office. It's how cops like us get as far as your buddy Alice has done.'

Leighton guessed that the captain clearly didn't know that Alice lived alone, but then she would probably want it that way.

'So, what about the missing girl and the car?' he asked.

'Like many young women, I reckon she may have simply ditched college when the pressure kicked in, and decided to head back to the safety of home.'

'What about the car?' Leighton asked. 'Why not just drive home?'

'How should I know?' the chief said with a shrug of his shoulders. Leighton could tell by his tone of voice that the captain was starting to get irritated. 'It could be any of a hundred reasons. Maybe she couldn't afford to up the cost of running a car and wanted to make a claim.'

'It's possible, I guess,' Leighton agreed reluctantly.

'It's not just possible,' the captain said confidently, 'it's also probable. Now get the hell out of here and let me get dressed.'

...

## 17

Leighton pulled his car into the street outside the small apartment he shared with Heather.

After clambering out of the car, with his arms full, he struggled to open the door whilst holding two warm pizza boxes and a bottle of wine. Getting dinner had taken him an hour longer than usual because, although here was a small pizzeria within walking distance of his apartment, he had found a small place closer to the harbour that sold a Quatro Staggioni that Heather had always liked when they used to spend more time at the beach. He could remember many summer evenings when the two of them would wander lazily, hand in hand, back from the surf to share dinner in the glow of a surfer café or pizza shack.

After Leighton knocked against it with his elbow, the door was finally opened by Heather. She was wearing jeans and a black sweater and holding a steaming plate of rice with a fork sticking out of it.

'Hey,' Leighton said, with a frown of confusion, 'didn't you remember I told you I would pick up dinner for us?'

'Yeah,' Heather said as she walked away from Leighton, leaving him to close the door with his foot and then follow her into the living area. She slumped down on one their two mismatched couches. The floor was littered with open textbooks. 'I wasn't sure when you would get back, so I figured I should just fix something. Otherwise I wouldn't be able to concentrate if was hungry.'

'You want to add a slice of pizza too? I've got plenty.' Leighton offered.

'No.' Heather shrugged. 'I'm good. You have it.'

'I got you the type you like,' Leighton added hopefully.

'I'm fat enough already,' Heather said without looking up from her own plate. This was an increasingly emerging theme, which Leighton's supportive comments did little to prevent.

'That's not true – you look great.' Leighton said. He meant it too.

'Whatever.' Heather sighed and continued eating her food. She continued to avoid looking at Leighton.

'I mean it.' he pressed.

'Yeah, well so do I,' Heather said firmly.

Leighton shrugged. walked into the small kitchen and grabbed a plate from a stack next to the sink. He flipped the square lid open on one of the pizza boxes, and pulled three slices on to his plate. The melted cheese stretched like elastic and Leighton pulled it with his fingers.

'You have a busy day?' he called through to the living area.

'Same old.' Heather called back.

'What did you get up to?'

'What do think?' she nodded at the floor. 'Reading mixed with a little reading.'

Leighton wandered into the room carrying his food and a glass of water. He stepped carefully through the books and papers as if crossing a field of landmines, before sinking into the opposite couch. He ate a slice of pizza, then considered the situation. The possibility of sitting in and relaxing with a bottle of wine seemed unlikely, but he still believed there was still a chance they might relax. 'You've been hitting the books a lot lately.'

'What's that supposed to mean?'

'Nothing bad. I was just thinking maybe you'd wanna take a break from it, grab a movie maybe?'

'Is there something you want to see?'

'No. I just mean both of us doing something other than work. Come on,' he grinned, 'just a couple of hours away from the paperwork.'

For a moment Heather hesitated as if she was considering the idea, but then promptly shook her head. 'No, I really need to get stuck into this. If I keep getting interrupted I won't get anywhere.'

Leighton sighed; he was nothing more than an interruption.

Heather's head snapped up. 'What's that noise supposed to mean?'

'I don't know,' Leighton shrugged. 'I guess it just seems that you have all day to do this. But when I come back you suddenly need to focus.'

'Suddenly?' Heather's voice rose in pitch. 'Yeah okay, whatever. Like I've been painting my nails all fucking day.'

'Look, I don't mean you're not focusing at other times'

'I don't want to speak about this.'

Leighton stood up and walked back into the kitchen. His appetite had slipped away.

The silence filling the apartment felt almost palpable.

The phone in the hallway rang. It seemed suddenly louder in the silent void. Heather made no move from the living area, so Leighton walked through and picked it up.

'Hello,' he said.

'Rookie, you busy?' It was Alice, her welcome voice seemed to be pulling Leighton up for air.

'No, I guess not.'

'Good, I'll pick you up outside your apartment in ten minutes.'

'I thought you were staying in the Holiday Inn in the city with your geriatric buddies?'

'I was meant to be, but some pencil pusher fucked up the booking – six of us were left off the list. Apparently my room won't be free until tomorrow. They offered to put me up in another hotel but the place was far out near the airport, so I figured I'd rather just head home to my own bed.'

'But you still going back there tomorrow?'

'Yeah, I'll have to head off at sunrise to get to the venue for our group breakfast. So, I just stopped in at the station when I heard about the latest discovery – I figured you'd be interested.'

'What's the *discovery*?' Leighton asked.

'You're just about to find out, Rookie,' Alice said and hung up.

When Leighton walked back into the room, Heather kept her eyes on her rice. 'Was that you getting an invite to go have some beers in your sweet little cop bar?' she asked without looking up.

'Yeah,' Leighton lied. He knew it wouldn't make any difference anyway. When Heather was like this, the fight was inevitable. If she thought Leighton was going to the bar, she would remain silent and disapproving until he left, but at least that meant there would be an escape for both of them.

It was ten minutes later-precisely- when Leighton watched Alice's dark green Duster pull up on the opposite side of the street He hurried across the two lanes and opened the car door.

'Hey partner,' Alice said cheerfully as Leighton climbed into the seat beside her. The vehicle was meticulously tidy inside, and a green plastic turtle air freshener was swinging from the rear view mirror like a tiny acrobat.

'Hey.' Leighton smiled in the hope of disguising his state of mind, but forgot he was sitting opposite a cop with thirty years under her belt.

'Everything okay with you, rookie?' she asked. Her tone indicated that she knew otherwise.

'Yeah, all good. Nice to have you back in town so soon.' Leighton said resolutely. 'So what's up?'

Alice nodded slowly. It was a gesture that indicated that she knew his claim of being *all good* was bullshit, but that she respected him enough to move on. 'We'll get there soon enough. How did you get on following up the owner of the Fiat?'

'Dead end,' Leighton said. 'Apparently, the owner's been missing from the college since Monday.'

'What's your gut say about it?' Alice asked.

'Hard to call.' Leighton said whilst rubbing his neck.

'Give it a shot,' Alice pushed.

'Okay, well she could've jacked-in college – those courses get harder every year and it's not the cheapest way to get ahead.'

'But you figure she's still alive, right?'

'Yeah,' Leighton shrugged, 'at least until a body shows up."

'Well, guess what, Rookie?' Alice asked.

'A body showed up?'

'Yep.'

'Our girl?'

'Possibly. Won't know till we get over there.'

'Where is *there*?'

'A sewage treatment place up at Windmill Canyon. You know it?'

Leighton shook his head. 'Nope – sewage treatment is not something I take an interest in. I see enough shit at work every day.'

'The place is nicer than it sounds,' Alice said as she pulled the car away from Leighton's apartment block. Both she and Leighton were oblivious to the fact they were being watched from the window of his home.

By the time Alice pulled up on North River Road there were already numerous emergency vehicles parked around the entrance to the remote water treatment facility. As she and

Leighton climbed out of the car, Alice called across the roof to him.

'So have you never even been up to this area before, Rookie?'

'No,' Leighton grinned, 'I don't like to know where everything goes after I flush.'

'Well, now you know. Come on.'

Alice led the way along the dusty road edge to the grand looking entrance to Whelan Lake. Tall palm trees stood like sentries on either side of two signs- one of which was pale blue and stated that the lake was a wild fowl nature reserve; the other indicated that part of the landscape was property of Oceanside Sewerage department.

The two officers walked through the entrance and turned onto a road leading down a gentle slope to two bodies of water. Halfway down the slope, a cruiser was parked sideways blocking any vehicles. The blue and red lights were flashing but nobody was in the car.

As they skirted by the car, Alice and Leighton were confronted by a young officer jogging up the road towards them.

'Hey you need to get out of here,' he called between breaths. 'This is an active crime scene!'

'Easy there, junior,' Alice pulled out her badge. 'I'm officer Alice Mead and this Leighton Jones. Who is the detective in charge down at the scene?'

'Jim Daniels,' the officer said, 'but he told me no-body was allowed through.'

'Well, I'll tell him that you tried to stop me, but short of shooting me nothing would work- and even that might not work. Come on Rookie.'

Alice and Leighton walked by the younger officer who bit his bottom lip and shook his head but made no move to stop them.

Up ahead was the familiar angular shape of a tow truck, and as they got closer to the water, Leighton got an overwhelming feeling of deja vu. A car was sitting at the edge of the small lake.

A detective wearing a cinnamon coloured suit came over to meet Alice and Leighton.

'Evening, Jim,' Alice said with more politeness than she would usually demonstrate.

'So d' you want to tell me what two off duty traffic cops are doing up here in the evening? You two up here on a date?'

'Yeah,' Alice said with a serious expression, 'but after making out with me on the back-seat for a couple of minutes, young Leighton here figured he'd rather see a dead body.'

Daniels chuckled and his grim expression softened. 'Why you really here, Alice?' Daniels asked. His tone was that of somebody eager to get on with the job.

'Two days ago, we pulled a similar car out the Buena Vista Lagoon. Did you hear about that at the station?'

'No,' Daniels said and suddenly appeared much less defensive. 'Anybody inside the vehicle?'

Alice turned to Leighton inviting him to contribute to the conversation.

'No- there wasn't.' Leighton said. 'But the owner – a young college student- has been M.I.A. since Monday.'

Daniels glanced briefly at Alice and then returned his attention to Leighton.

'So,' Alice began, 'I was hoping that maybe` you'd share what you've got just in case there's some kind of connection between your discovery and ours.'

For a moment, the detective looked away from Alice and Leighton. It seemed that he was possibly about to clam up, but then he turned to Alice and sighed.

'Jesus! Okay, I'll give you five minutes. Get your asses over here but touch nothing. I've had a hard enough job trying to preserve the scene as it is.'

Daniels walked away leaving Alice and Leighton to hurry after him. He led them to the vehicle, which had all four doors open. A crime scene technician and a photographer were each engaged in the business of gathering their own respective evidence. They moved around each other in some symbiotic dance, each giving way to the other when required. The focus of their attention was the corpse of a young woman slumped in the drivers' seat.

'What's the story?' Alice asked.

'A worker from the water plant came over here for a smoke about 10.30 this morning. He said he noticed the roof of the car just beneath the surface. He figured it was perhaps a sign that had blown down into the water, but he said when the sun light shifted he could see the whole shape of a car. He called his supervisor and the came over here with a couple of industrial pumps. After a few hours, they had drained enough of the water to confirm that the object was a car and that somebody was inside it. That was when we got the call.'

'Female, Caucasian, early twenties. No ID as yet. We ran the plates. Car is part of a hire fleet from a place on Langford Street. There's been no report of a stolen vehicle so it seems like the driver most likely had hired it. We need to wait until the place opens tomorrow morning to confirm the details.'

'You got a probable cause of death yet?'

'Nothing apparent- so we need to see what the autopsy comes back with. What was the story with the driver of your car?'

'Female, Caucasian early twenties, 'Alice said, 'in fact she's pretty much like your girl sitting over there in the driver's seat. Might even be the same person – or whoever put her in the water has a particular type. '

'Shit. Somebody needs to radio the station and get that car locked down- it could easily be a potential crime scene.'

'I already did that. I was leaving the station when I heard dispatch discussing the discovery up here. It seemed a little too coincidental, so I asked Gary Deans at the garage to tape up and secure the Fiat.'

'Good call,' Daniels said.

Leighton, who was peering intently into the wet vehicle, turned to look at Daniels. 'Was the driver's mirror in that position when you pulled the car out?'

Daniels bent slightly and looked into the car. 'You mean was it twisted around like that?'

Leighton nodded.

'Yeah, it must've been. We've only touched the glovebox and the girl's possessions.'

Whilst Leighton was speaking, Alice had turned her attention to the surrounding area. She gazed around in all directions and then turned back to face Daniels. 'Seems like a nice spot to park up and take in the view or maybe take a dog for a walk. Were there any witnesses in the area last night?'

'One of my uniforms spoke to a couple of kids who were hanging around the entrance on their BMX's. They said that they saw a red car in the area but couldn't confirm make or model.'

Leighton glanced at Alice.

'Okay,' Daniels shrugged, 'as you can clearly see my team has some work to do here, so feel free to stick around, but if the captain shows up looking for an explanation, you two are carrying the can on your own.'

'It's okay, Jim- we just wanted to share the details.'

'Well, I appreciate it. But now, if you don't mind, piss off.'

'Will do,' Alice said, 'you have a good one.'

Alice led Leighton away from the car with the dead girl inside.

'Your buddy back there is a real prince!' Leighton said as he walked back to the car.

'Who- Daniels? He's alright,' Alice said. 'Working Homicide just dulls your people skills after a while. They spend their time looking at the worst things that people do to other people. I guess it leaves them a little less friendly than us cheery traffic cops.'

'So it seems.'

'Well, there's no need to worry about it, Rookie. Nobody from Traffic ever moves across to Homicide, so hopefully you'll hopefully manage to retain your unique charm throughout your career.'

'I hope so,' Leighton chuckled. 'So what's the next move?'

'I guess that it depends on what the M.E. Says – if they confirm that the girl in that car back there was murdered, then there's a good chance that our girl is dead too.'

'So, we just wait?' Leighton sounded disappointed.

'Yeah, unless our missing girl shows up back in her college class tomorrow morning.' Alice shrugged her shoulders as if it was a possibility, but Leighton knew the truth from her tone of voice that it wasn't a likely one.

'But you don't believe she will, do you?'

'No, I don't.' Alice said with a tinge of sadness in her voice.

'Me neither,' Leighton said, 'funny that.'

By now they had reached the top of the slope. As they walked back through the entrance to the water plant, Leighton stopped and gazed around at the slow curves of the surrounding hills. Somewhere in the distance, the ocean was melting into the evening sky. Alice took a couple of steps forward then noticed her partner was no longer by her side. She stopped and turned back towards Leighton.

'Hey what's the matter?' she called to him.

Leighton continued to gaze around. 'Just taking a look at his place. I've never come up to this part of the city, so I never knew how nice it is up here.'

'Yeah, it really is.' Alice said as she stepped closer to Leighton. 'I used to live in a condo not far from here in Whelan Ranch. Of course that was back when I was young and dumb. Paid over the odds in rent for two years – nice view though.'

Keeping her eyes on the horizon, Alice spoke directly to Leighton. 'So, is the natural beauty of this place the only thing on your mind, Rookie or is there anything else bothering you?'

There was a moment of silence during which Alice turned and looked at the sadness in Leighton's eyes. She knew what she wanted him to say. It had been obvious to her that for some time now he was having a really tough time at home, but he had always attempted to keep his personal problems hidden. Despite his relative youth, Leighton had a quiet dignity that held his troubles back from his mouth. When Alice had first started working with him, Leighton had lost his father a month earlier. Sometimes when they had been out on patrol, she would notice him look at certain white haired guys driving by and a flicker of sudden emotion would cross his face. It appeared as if he had thought for a moment that his dad had returned and was simply driving along the Boulevard. On the first couple of times this occurred, Alice would check in and ask if he was okay, but after Leighton's insistence that he was fine, she let it slide. He was a private and dignified young man.

In recent months, however. it was no longer white haired men who elicited a wistful and lost look from Alice's partner – it was happy looking couples.

'Yeah,' Leighton said with an unconvincing smile, 'just admiring the view.'

'Glad to hear it. Now mover your ass, rookie I'll take you home. Some of us need to take an early drive in the morning.'

'You mean you don't fancy cycling along the Interstate to San Diego?' Leighton asked.

Alice laughed as they reached her parked car. 'Yeah, maybe if I wanted to reach the Holiday Inn for suppertime.'

By the time Leighton returned home, it was 10.22 pm – not particularly late, but the apartment he shared with Heather was already dark and silent. As he entered the small hallway, he noticed that the bedroom door was firmly shut.

He walked into the kitchen hoping to perhaps grab a slice of cold pizza, but he found that both boxes and their contents had been crushed into the plastic trash can.

Leighton quietly took off his shoes and then walked softly into the living room where he sat down on the neat couch. When he reached across and switched on a small table lamp, he discovered a piece of notepaper lying on the wooden coffee table. Leighton sighed and picked it up. There were only four words: *Sleeping – keep noise down*. No name, no kiss, just a simple instruction. After, scrunching up the paper, Leighton reached back to the lamp and switched it off. He then lay down on the couch. It was a small space, but if he curled up, he could fit himself into it. It wouldn't be the first time.

As the room began sinking into darkness, Leighton looked to the window, where he could see into the apartments on the other side of the street. The many squares windows were illuminated by warm light, and therefore offered glimpses of couples watching TV together or sharing some take- out food, whilst simply talking and laughing. After looking at them for a moment, Leighton felt like an intruder so shifted his gaze to the visible shaft of sky above the apartments where the sky was fading from purple to black.

Eventually, he closed his eyes and slipped into darkness himself.

## 18

As soon as Leighton arrived at Oceanside Police headquarters, he parked up then crossed the sunlit parking lot and approached the staff entrance, which was located at the rear of the station. A younger officer – David Hare – who often covered reception from 7am till noon was standing smoking a cigarette at the side of the cream coloured building. Hundreds of crushed stubs lay scattered around the ground at the officer's feet. They always reminded Leighton of 9mm shell casings. He figured they were probably just as lethal.

Leighton had just raised a hand in greeting as they passed, when the other officer called to him.

'Hey Jonesy, some young punk showed up at reception looking to speak to you about half an hour ago?'

'To speak to me?' Leighton frowned. 'Are you sure about that?'

'Yeah, we've only one Jones on the books.' Hare said and then sucked on the final half inch of his cigarette, screwing his eyes up against the smoke.

'Did this guy leave his name?' Leighton asked.

'There was no need for that,' the other officer said as he dropped the butt on the ground and then crushed it under the heel of his shoe, 'he's still in reception waiting for you.'

'Thanks,' Leighton said and then entered into the cool shade of the station building.

Leighton walked through the locker room, passed admin and then the dispatch room. He then turned left and entered the spacious tiled reception area of Oceanside Police station, to where a nervous looking young man was sitting at the end of a row of orange plastic chairs. Above the young man's head was a large poster of two cannabis joints overlapping each other to form a cross. The phrase 'Just Say No!' was printed beneath the cross in large black letters. It was a message that in recent months had been repeated not only throughout the station, but across the entire country.

As Leighton approached him, he noticed that the teenage visitor was holding a dog-eared copy of a Piers Anthony novel. The way in which the kid's feet were tapping told Leighton that the guy was either stressed about something or had taken too many coffees from the complimentary machine in the foyer – possibly both.

'Hi, I'm officer Jones. I heard you were hoping to speak to me, is that right?'

The young man looked up hopefully. 'You're the one looking into Kelly's disappearance?'

"Yeah, I am. How did you get my name?'

'I asked Dale who works on reception. The dude couldn't remember your name but luckily he had written the details on a pad behind the counter. I guess there's no intelligence test for wardens.'

'So you know Kelly. Are you a friend of hers? Leighton asked.

'Yeah, well not like a friend I guess. I mean I'd like to be.' The young man dropped his head, and then placed the book in his lap and ran the fingers of both hands through his overgrown hair.

Leighton sat down in a chair alongside the young man. 'Look. why don't you take your time and then tell me what brought you here this morning, okay?'

The young man nodded.

'Yeah, right. Okay, so like I said I was playing pool in the social area of the student resident block when I heard you asking about Kelly.'

Leighton raised his eyebrows.

'Let's start with your name, which is what?'

'Corey Troy.'

'Okay, Corey, if you're not Kelly's friend, how do you know her?'

'It's nothing weird. Honestly. We both work the same shifts at the natatorium.'

'What is that- a bar or club?'

Troy laughed. 'No sir, it's the indoor pool for the sports team students on scholarships. Kinda like a private pool for the serious swimmers or those on the swim team.'

'Ah,' Leighton nodded, 'so you and Kelly are colleagues?'

'Yeah, we have been working together since the start of the year, which kinda makes us work buddies. I had my name down to work in the commons kitchens but I passed my lifeguard test back in June so I got lucky.'

Leighton noticed how the guy couldn't help but smile when he talked about Kelly. 'So are you guys pretty close?' he asked.

'Well, during our shifts we have to sit on these tall lookout chairs at either end of the water, so it's hard to chat to each other, you know?'

Leighton nodded. He could see the kid was genuinely sad.

'But, a couple of times each shift, we have to switch places. Like, I go to the bottom end of the pool and she comes over to the top area. That's my favourite part of the shift – when Kelly walks up the poolside towards me and we pass each other. We always just goof around- high-five each other that kind of thing. She's just cooler than anyone else I know.

'So you *really* like her then?'

'Yeah, but even though we work at the same place, we are kind of always out of sync. I guess I've been working up to asking her out for a date.

The young man stopped speaking and looked down at his hands, which gripped the paperback novel as if it was a survival manual. Leighton followed his gaze and noticed the well- used condition of the paperback.

'So, you're a bit of a bookworm then?' he asked.

'Yeah,' the boy seemed to brighten as he spoke.'

'What's your favourite?'

'I like some horror but fantasy adventure books mostly- pretty much any story that takes you off to another world.'

Leighton could already see that. He suspected that Kelly barely knew that this guy even existed.

'Well, look Corey a crush on a fellow student?'

'No, that's not it.' The young man adjusted the book in his lap and then rubbed his hands together and looked them intently. 'I mean I do like her, but it's not just that.'

'So, tell me what else is on your mind.'

'Okay,' Corey nodded and then took a breath. 'On Friday morning, I finally worked up the courage to ask Kelly for a date. I just figured maybe it was the right time. Only, there was a problem.'

'What was that?'

'There had been a shift change and so she wasn't working that morning. I was kind of bummed out as you can imagine. Anyway, I saw her later in the day coming out of an American Lit class. It was pretty busy and she was a few steps ahead of me in the crowd. So, I walked a little faster, you know trying to catch up with her but it was tough pushing against everyone else as they hurried to classes.'

Leighton nodded.

'Anyway, I could kind of see Kelly heading for the door leading to the rear parking lot. That's a place only ever used by college staff – you need to have permit otherwise you'll get clamped and have to pay forty bucks to get it removed, but I guess that's the only way to stop students using it.'

'Did you follow her?'

'Yeah, sorry. I went through the door and I figured I could catch up with her, and it might even be easier to ask for a date with nobody else around.'

'So you actually spoke to her that day?' Leighton asked.

Corey shook his head. 'No sir, I didn't actually get the chance to.'

'How come?'

'Well, I reached the exit a couple of minutes after Kelly, but by the time I got outside she had totally vanished. It kinda messed with my head, you know- I was sure I had seen her but then for a couple of moments I was starting to doubt myself.'

'So that was it – she just vanished?'

'No, I stayed there at the back of the building to have a smoke?'

Leighton raised his eyebrows.

'Jeez, it was just a cigarette- okay?'

Leighton nodded in acceptance, but he suspected the kid was lying – at least about the smoke if nothing else.

'Anyway, as I was lighting up I looked up and realised where Kelly had gone to.'

'And where was that?'

'She was sitting in the passenger seat of a blue Toyota at the back of the parking lot.'

'Was she alone?'

'No,' Corey shook his head and frowned, 'she was with a guy, and they were having one hell of a loud fight. I mean I was at least a couple of cars away and I could hear them at it. I mean the windows were open, but it was still pretty loud.'

'So were you able to hear what this fight was about?'

'Yeah partly.' The young man nodded. 'She was telling him to pretty much back off.'

'Back off from what?'

'Her, I guess. I mean it sounded like she was telling him to stay the fuck away from her. Sorry! I mean she was telling him to keep away.'

'It's okay,' Leighton said. 'You carry on, don't worry about curse words.'

'Well, it didn't sound like he was listening. He kept saying that he cared deeply. What a freak!'

'What happened after you saw them?'

'Well. I wasn't sure if things were going to turn ugly, so I crossed the parking lot, just as if I was cutting through it on my way to class, but getting close enough to the Toyota so they knew I was there. By the time I reached the other side of the lot, I glanced back and saw Kelly get out of the car.'

'Was she okay?'

'Yeah, but judging by how hard she slammed the door, I'd say she was pretty pissed.'

'Did the guy make any attempt to follow her?'

'No he just sat in the car – not driving or anything, more like he was thinking.'

'Joel do you think you would you recognise the guy again if you saw him?'

'Hell, of course I would.' Corey laughed.' Everyone would.'

'What do you mean- do you know who the man with Kelly was?'

'Oh yeah,' the young man looked suddenly excited, 'but here's the thing. He isn't one of the students; he's one of the tutors- a guy called Marc Nichols.'

'A teacher?'

'Yeah, he's not like as old as some of the staff, but yeah he's one of our American Literature lecturers.'

'Okay. Do you reckon there was possibly something going on between Kelly and this guy Nichols?'

'Yeah, totally!' Corey nodded vigorously. 'When I first started working at the swimming pool, I told one of the girls who worked in the front desk that I was thinking of asking Kelly out for a date. She just laughed and told me I was about twenty years too young for her. At the time, I'd just shrugged it off as her messing, but when I saw Kelly in the car with Nichols, I realised that the girl had been right. I realised that he is always using at the gym next to the pool- probably trying to get close to her. And then I showed up for work this morning and some guy was working Kelly's shift because she's still not around.'

'Okay,' Leighton said. 'Thanks for coming down here. I want you to know that you did the right thing letting me know about this.'

'Well, I just figured that maybe, she decided to jack the whole college thing in just to get away from the creep.'

Leighton nodded. That scenario, he believed, might be one of the better potential outcomes. 'How did you get over here today?' Leighton asked.

Corey shrugged. 'I took a couple of buses.'

'So will you be heading back to the campus now?'

'Yeah,' the young man sighed, 'I have to hit the library – there's a paper due tomorrow, and I'm on early pool duty so I need to get it done tonight.'

Come on then,' Leighton stood up, 'I'll drive you back to college, and see if I can have chat with your lecturer.'

## 19

After dropping off Corey Troy at the entrance to the Coley Library – a building which resembled a squat white fort- Leighton parked his cruiser and walked along paths to the commons building. The afternoon was hotter outside than expected and Leighton wished he had picked up a bottle of water.

As he passed by various students who were sitting smoking, reading or both on benches outside the entrance, Leighton realised that almost all of them seemed happy. He glanced at them and smiled, envying their possibility and the potential to shape their lives. Despite being in his mid-twenties, Leighton was already feeling that his life had somehow drifted out of his control and he didn't know how to get it back again.

Eventually, he arrived at the building. After pushing through the glass door, Leighton descended a flight of stone stairs to the administration level, and then walked up to the desk where a neatly dressed woman was sitting typing frantically into a bulky computer. A cream coloured telephone handset was wedged between her chin and shoulder. As Leighton approached the counter, she smiled and held up one manicured finger. Leighton nodded and waited patiently.

'Okay,' she said into the handset, 'I've typed that in but it makes no difference.'

She paused for a moment, then tapped some more keys. 'Okay,' she said, 'that seems to have worked – for now at least. Thanks Karen. You have a nice day.'

The receptionist replaced the telephone handset then looked at Leighton and smiled.

'Hi, sorry to keep you, officer. These dumb new computers are more trouble than their worth. I don't know what is wrong with a good old-fashioned typewriter.'

'I hear you,' Leighton said knowingly.

'So what can we do for you?'

'My name is Leighton Jones from Oceanside PD. I was hoping to speak to a member of staff who teaches here– at least I believe he does.'

'Sure. We have a couple of senior staff offices in this building, but at this time of day they might be teaching and we have a pretty wide campus. So you may need to take a trek to one of the lecture halls to find them.'

'That's fine with me-it's a nice day out there.'

'Okay, well luckily we still have paper timetables – so I don't need to fight with HAL here.,' she shot an accusative look at the silent computer. 'What is the name of the staff member you're looking for?'

'Marc Nichols,' Leighton said, 'I think he lectures humanities.

'Yeah, I think he does – only joined us a couple of years ago. Give me a second.' The receptionist began to rifle through the various sheets of paper. Then suddenly she stopped and frowned. A small sheet of pink paper was stapled to one of the timetables. 'Looks like it's not your day officer.'

'What's wrong?' Leighton asked.

'It seems that Mr Nichols has taken two weeks of leave.'

'Since when?'

'Let me see.' The receptionist peered at the paper. 'Yeah the request form is stamped here from Monday.'

'Is it normal for a lecturer to take a break in the middle of a semester?' Leighton asked.

'No, not as far as I know. Not unless they were ill, or maybe experienced a death of somebody close to them.'

Leighton tried to not let the receptionist see that this scenario was exactly what he was afraid of, but she was already looking a little rattled. She had one hand pressed against her forehead.

'You okay, ma'am?'

'Yeah,' she said faintly, 'I just remembered something.'

'Remembered what?' Leighton asked.

'Look, you didn't hear this from me, right?' She glanced over her shoulder as if checking for anyone close enough to hear.

'Sure,' Leighton said and nodded. 'I'll keep your name out of it.'

The receptionist took a deep breath as if she was about to dive into water, and then she spoke in a conspiratorial whisper. 'My cousin Betty works in the administration over at UCLA. She's been there for sixteen years – doesn't need the money either. Her husband, Richard, is a big shot accountant. So she only works to get her out of her big empty house. Anyway, Betty told me that when Marc Nichols first started here it was because he had been in some kind of trouble at her college.' She used her two index fingers to make inverted commas when she said the word 'trouble'.

'Okay, I get you,' Leighton said quietly. 'You have any idea what kind of trouble he was in?'

'I'm honestly not one hundred percent sure, but heard it was something to do with him being involved in an inappropriate romance. And so now he's suddenly taking leave in the middle of a semester. Seems a little weird huh?'

'Yeah,' Leighton nodded, 'it does seem that way. Do you happen to have a home address on record for Mr Nichols?'

'Sure, but I'll have to write out by hand until Robbie the Robot here decides to play nicely.'

'Hand-written is totally fine with me,' Leighton said with a smile.

Whilst the woman was scribbling down details on a piece of paper, Leighton was already anticipating a number of possible scenarios linked to the sudden departure or Mr Nichols. It was quite possible this guy could have abducted Kelly and be holding her prisoner, or he might have done something and decided to get out of town. The former seemed more likely than the latter, but in either case, Leighton was determined to find him.

# 20

Leighton was sitting at one of the three small cramped desks which were allocated to the six members of Traffic Division. They were located in a back corner of the office area, beneath an erratic strip light which bussed and flickered in little bursts every hour or so. During the afternoon, the station offices were fairly quiet. Most officers on day shifts, would be out on the streets until around 5pm when they would return to complete any necessary paperwork before change-over. However, on the days when educational classes such as driver awareness were running, a smattering of officers would make use of the office space as well as the small station canteen.

Having devoured his lunch (a turkey sub and a tepid black coffee), Leighton was using two fingers to clumsily type into a yellow form when the telephone on his desk rang. It was rare for anyone to call directly through to the desk, so Leighton picked up the handset with a degree of trepidation.

'Hello, Oceanside P.D- can I help you?' he said.

'Hey, Rookie,' said a familiar voice, 'are you missing me?'

'Of course,' Leighton said with a grin, 'It's been almost twenty-four hours, and I've got nobody here to buy coffee for. So you learning anything on that *Golden Girls* course with your new retirement buddies?'

'The only thing I've learned is to avoid the buffet – I'm sure some of that alleged food has been sitting out on the hotplates for more than a week.' Alice sighed and Leighton thought he could sense she was tired- or perhaps even a little lonely. 'So, you make any progress with the car in the lagoon?' she asked.

'Well, I discovered that the owner of the Fiat has been missing since Monday. Her dorm buddy over at USD confirmed that she hasn't shown up for any of her college classes or for work?'

'Anyone submitted a Missing Person's report yet?'

'Just me.' Leighton said. 'Next of kin is listed in the college paperwork as a grandparent in Nebraska. It might suggest she hasn't got anyone else.'

'I know how that feels,' Alice said with a low chuckle. 'Who was working the admin desk when you submitted in the report?'

'Len Freeman.'

'That's good- Len's a reliable guy- he'll get it processed straight away. So at least that puts the kid in the system. Do we know anything else?'

'Yeah, and this is the one that concerns me-apparently just before she vanished Kelly was seen in an altercation with one of her college teachers.'

'When was this?'

'On Friday. It happened off the grid too – in a parking lot at the rear of the campus buildings.'

'I'd say you're probably right to be concerned-that doesn't sound too good.'

'I'm not finished- it gets better.' Leighton said with a nervous laugh.

'Tell me.'

'So, I took a drive over the college to speak to the guy she was seen with. However, when I asked about the guy at the college reception, I was told that he's currently absent. Apparently, the guy suddenly decided to take two weeks of unplanned vacation.'

'Shit!' Leighton heard Alice blow out a stream of air.

'Your reaction sounds like my own,' he said. 'Doesn't sound good, does it?'

'Not by a mile. Did you pass on your concerns to the captain?' Alice asked.

'Well, I tried.'

'What does that mean?'

'I told him everything I had, and he told me it sounded like a big fat nothing. I felt like he wanted to pat my head, give me a popsicle and push me out of the office.'

'Fuck that!' Alice said loudly. 'The whole thing stinks. We all know the department is under pressure to be seen to be tackling the drugs coming across the south-west border but does that mean we ignore everything else to keep the pencil pushers in city hall happy?'

'I get it. But I'm working next weekend, so I'm off shift for the next two days. There's not much I can do.''

'You got an address for this college lecturer?'

'Yeah,' Leighton said happily, 'funnily enough I just pulled it from DMV.'

'Well, what are you waiting for?'

'What do you mean - you want me to go knock on the guy's door?'

'Shit, Rookie, I don't want you to send him a bunch of flowers! In any case, if you pulled his home address off the files I reckon you were probably planning on heading over there anyway – so don't make like this was all my idea.'

'You got me,' Leighton laughed. 'Okay, I'll take a drive over there, visit the address and check out the home.'

'If you feel like you're not getting anywhere, tell him that he could be charged with obstruction.'

'We can do that?'

'Sure, you'd only be stating a fact.' Alice said, 'plus you'll be amazed how easy it is to flip a reluctant witness with the threat of jail.'

'You never fail to amaze me, officer Mearns. How do you know this stuff?'

'I worked Vice before moving to traffic?'

'So why did you make the shift?'

'Well,' Alice said pensively, 'I guess I had made up my mind to retire at fifty-five, and I wanted to have a less dramatic couple of years?'

'Didn't really pan out that way did it?' Leighton laughed.

'Indeed it did-fucking-not.  Anyway, you just stay under the radar when approaching the place. If he's our guy, he may choose to bug out if he senses law enforcement are sniffing around him.  I'll check in with you tomorrow- that's if the terrible food in this place doesn't get to me first.'

## 21

The afternoon sun was baking the streets as Leighton parked his car outside the neat, peach-coloured building on the outskirts of the city. The single storey residence was bordered by a low wall and featured a small Zen garden formed of raked gravel and a couple of neatly placed rocks. In the garden of the adjoining property, an elderly woman wearing a wide brimmed sun hat was standing on a metal step ladder whilst pruning a large Californian Holly. She glanced up as Leighton drew nearer, then busied herself with removing dead flower heads.

As he approached the red door, Leighton thought it appropriate to indicate that he was not about to break down the door, so gave a small smile and a nod to the neighbour who tipped her head politely. The gesture reminded Leighton of how a cowboy might greet a stranger in town.

Reaching the door of the property, Leighton raised one hand towards a white plastic button located on the edge of the wooden frame.

'There's no need to ring the buzzer, officer?' the neighbour called across to Leighton. Turning sideways to follow the sound of her voice, Leighton found the woman now standing next to the ladder and holding the shears in her hands.

'Excuse me?' he said.

'There's no point in you wasting your time standing there waiting for an answer. Mr Nichols is not at home at the moment. Are you a friend of his?'

'No, I'm here professionally. I'm just following up on a traffic incident.'

The woman lowered the shears in a subconscious act of truce.

'Not his fault, I hope. He's such a nice man.'

'Well, I'm really just looking for some information,' Leighton nodded towards the house, 'Do you have any idea when Mr Nichols might return?'

The elderly woman shook her head very seriously. 'Probably not for a couple of days I imagine.'

'What makes you think that?' Leighton asked.

'Well this week I've been out in the garden most days. I've not really been planting anything – not at this time of year- more just trying to tidy things up a little. And some of the storms we had last week damn near killed off half my succulents. Anyway, being out here means I see everything. So on Tuesday – or maybe Monday, I saw Marc pack up the car with a few bags of groceries and a suitcase.'

'Did you speak to him?'

'No, he was wearing those damned headphones that all the kids seem to have nowadays.'

'Any idea where he might have been heading?'

'To the cabin I expect.' The way the woman said this made it sound as if Leighton should already have known this.

'Cabin?'

'Yes- he calls it his Shangri-la – I imagine that it serves as his escape from all the college stuff and all those hippy students." The woman's expression suddenly changed as if she had tasted something unpleasant. 'In all honesty I couldn't do his job – not even if you paid me a million dollars. It's just far too stressful working with young people many of whom will be high on drugs, but I expect that's why he goes up to the cabin.'

'I don't suppose you know where this cabin is located, do you?'

'Oh yes,' the woman said as she nodded, 'of course. It's on the northern side of Bear Lake. It used to belong to his parents but when they passed away, Marc took it on as a project. I advised him on which plants would last best up there in his cabin in between visits. If you don't opt for succulents, they will just wither and die.'

Leighton nodded respectfully. 'Thank you for taking the time to speak to me. You've been very helpful.'

'It's my pleasure,' the woman smiled and stepped back on to her ladder again. 'If you manage to catch up with Marc, can you tell that him I'll water his rose bushes until he gets back? Don't want him worrying if we get another dry spell, especially if the stress has been getting to him.'

'I will do. You have nice day,' Leighton said and then turned and walked to his car. On the way hoped that neglected plants would be the only things which were at risk of dying at the hands of Marc Nichols.'

## 22

On the way back from the Nichols' place, Leighton's mind was filled with a powerful memory from six years earlier. At the time, he and Heather had spent much more time in each other's company. They didn't have much money, but still managed to create something almost idyllic. Entire weeks were spent lazing together on the beach or hiking on the trails around Oceanside. On one occasion they had driven a battered red Toyota to Bear Lake and camped overnight on the shore.

After pulling on their back packs, he and Heather had locked up the car and then stepped on to a magical path through the fragrant woods. Leighton could remember how closely connected the two of them had seemed as they wandered in step with each other along the trail. On wider paths, they would hold each other's hands; on more narrow sections, they would take turns to lead the way through the wilderness. When Leighton had been in front, Heather had joked that she was distracted by seeing sexy muscles on his legs. They had chatted about books and movies and nothing for hours. Occasionally, they would stop to share a bottle of water and admire the scenery. Leighton smiled to himself when he remembered how Heather would often turn, wrap her arms around him and softly kiss his mouth.

That evening they found a quiet clearing, and goofed around whilst setting up the tent. Afterwards, Leighton and Heather sat beside in the warm glow of the sweet smelling campfire and, feasted on bread and cheese and cheap red wine. Afterwards, they had drifted into the tent and peeled off each other's clothes. Leighton had drowned in pleasure as their warm, toned bodies moved together in a slow shared rhythm.

Later Leighton and Heather lay together, gazing contentedly out of the triangular doorway watching the tiny flickers of gold floating up from the smouldering fire into the ink coloured sky. Heather had quietly fallen asleep, breathing softly, but Leighton had remained awake watching the slow dance of the orange sparks, foolishly believing his happiness would somehow never end.

Eventually, Leighton pulled his car over next to a roadside payphone and climbed out of his car. After slotting a couple of coins into a groove in the metal box, he punched in the numbers and held the glossy black handset to his ear. It smelled of the previous caller's cheap perfume. The telephone rang for a moment before it was picked up at the other end of the line.

'Hello?' Heather answered. Her voice sounded okay- not cheerful – but still okay.

'Hi,' Leighton said, 'it's just me. What you up to?'

'Nothing much – I've just been reading a report all morning.'

'A report?'

'Yeah, it's called A Nation at Risk.'

'So how was it?'

'Hard to say-I'm only a little way through it. So why are you calling up in the middle of the day?' Leighton could hear that there was simmering irritation in Heather's tone but it was still at a fairly low level.

'Well, I'm following up a lead at work and it turns out that I need to take a drive up to Bear Lake, I thought you might want to tag along.'

'Bear Lake! Why the hell are you going there?'

'Just following a lead on a car we found sunk down in the Buena Vista Lagoon. So do you want to?'

'Want to what?'

'Tag along?' Leighton asked hopefully.

'No Leighton, I've got to get through this stuff.' Heather sighed audibly, 'I know you really don't get it, but I really need to learn this stuff if I want to teach kindergarten.'

'Hey, that's not fair- I do get it,' Leighton said.

'You do?'

'Yeah, I think so.'

'Well then why would you be trying to take me away from my studies to go on some crazy drive-'

'Come on, I wasn't trying to put you off.'

'No?' Heather didn't sound convinced.

'Why would I?'

'I don't know – why would you?'

Leighton suddenly felt that his last hike had been with someone else entirely and that it had taken place a thousand years earlier.

'I just thought it would be nice for you to get out of the apartment for a couple of hours. I just figured that maybe it would be good for you.'

Heather sighed audibly. 'Do you know what would be good for me? Some peace would be good for me.'

'Okay,' Leighton bit his lip and nodded.

'You sound pissed off. Don't be like that!' Heather said.

'Look, I'm going to get going. I'll see you when I get back from the Lake.;

'Leighton.'

Hey hung up.

# 23

At 1. 43 pm Oceanside beach was relatively quiet. During school term there were fewer kids and families on the sand. There were always a few surfers, slicing over the tumbling waves, but the shoreline was usually clear and that was how Debbie Walker like it when she took her daily jog on the beach. At thirty-eight years old, she was still keen to stay in shape, her partner Steph often told her she looked great, but Debbie had often seen her casting appreciate glances at the some of their more toned neighbours. Steph herself was no oil painting but she wasn't burdened with Debbie's lack of confidence.

When she had initially started running on the side-walks and roads Debbie found that the repeated impact had begun to hurt her knees. The pain had almost been enough to make her quit this form of exercise completely. She tried running on the sand closest to the path, but it was soft and powdery and made running almost impossible. However, in time she had discovered that just after the tide had gone out the sand was compact enough to offer a firm surface, but it also created less of a shock on her joints.

The route she liked best was one which MiDebbie would take most days. When it wasn't too busy, she would usually park her Jeep in front of the colourful surf shop near Carlsbad beach, which was an ideal location for Debbie. She liked the convenience of being close to the nearby Carlsbad Beach Restrooms as it was much easier to run with an empty bladder than with a full one. From the surf shop it was a small hop down to the shore.

The daily route usually would take Debbie all the way along Tamarack Beach to the wide neck of the lagoon. At that point, the beach was split by the wide body of water and large jagged rocks fringed the large flow into the sea. Faced with this barrier, Debbie would cut up the side of the lagoon on to the coastal trail, and then run upon a neat path which ran alongside the gleaming railway line all the way to Walnut Avenue. This left Debbie with little more than a short hop on to the street which then led back to the surf shop. The looping route was only a couple of miles but it was enough to keep Debbie in shape and best of all it was free of traffic.

At first she thought the strange shape on the rocks was a mannequin. It was understandable. In the six months Debbie had been taking an early morning run, she had seen all sorts of random trash thrown down from the four lane boulevard above. On one memorable occasion, she had discovered two burst cartons of rainbow coloured pinatas crushed on the rocks. The scene had reminded Debbie of a disturbing painting she had once seen featuring a tangle of dead buffalo driven over the edge of a cliff.

But this time a strange internal alarm was telling Debbie that today's discovery was different from the other random debris. Most objects would catch her attention for a moment as she ran by them but none of them triggered any kind of emotional response – except perhaps irritation at the selfishness of some people. Today was different; the shape on the rocks unsettled Debbie in a profound way that she struggled to understand.

She had been running along the coffee coloured shore line, listening to *When Doves Cry* on her red Sony *Walkman* when Debbie had glanced in the direction of the beach path and first noticed the bizarre object.

The sloped bluff descending from the four lanes of the boulevard down which overlooked the beach was only about thirty feet high but steep and rocky. At the foot of the slope was a long concrete cycle path, which ran the length of the beach. This stone channel was walled on either side and was popular with cyclists, young mums, and the occasional roller-skater. It was in the rocky ground above this path that the object

Halfway down the bluff, on a ledge that would be unseen from the path below was what appeared to be some sort of pale mannequin. Yet the figure was entirely upside down with head facing the beach and feet pointing back to the road above. This posture gave the impression that the mannequin was climbing down to the water, and in the years which followed her discovery Debbie would often dream that it was doing just that- crawling towards her.

Stopping for a moment, her chest rising and falling, Debbie stood with her hands on hips and looked towards the rocky slope. She narrowed her eyes in an attempt to focus, but at a distance of twenty or so yards away it was difficult to see. In the blue sky above the woman, gulls were starting to screech as if sounding an alarm. Debbie held a hand up to shield her eyes from the sun and peered more intently at the object. In her mind she was trying to explain it away, as if that would calm the uncomfortable sensation which was unfolding in her stomach. Perhaps, she thought, it was an inflatable doll thrown over the edge as a college prank, or it could be a cardboard cut-out of a famous person like the ones they sometimes had in her local Blockbuster video store.

Without fully being aware of what she was doing, Debbie began to take slow steps towards the rocky slope. At that initial point, she had been confused because a regular stream of bikers and joggers were passing along the path beneath the object, so it seemed unlikely that it was anything alarming.

Then as she grew closer, Debbie realised why nobody else was concerned by the sight. The location of the object was lying on a rocky shelf, which was concealed by protrusions lower down in the sandstone slope. This meant that people moving along the path in the sunshine by were blissfully aware of the strange form lying upside-down a few feet above their heads.

By the time Debbie reached the cycle path, her view of the object was obscured by the rock-face, which sloped upwards above her. She immediately jogged backwards on the powdery sand until she could glimpse it again. However, by that point she was so far back to make accurate identification of the object impossible. At that moment in time, Debbie was utterly fixated on her weird discovery and unable to let it go. Biting her bottom lip, she made a mental note of the features of the cliff- a couple of holes and fissures in the bluff directly below the mannequin- that were easy to recognise. Debbie knew that by keeping a visual fix on these points, she could return to the path with an idea of approximately where the thing lay.

Debbie then walked carefully and deliberately back across the beach towards the path. As her feet sank into the softer sand, she kept her eyes fixed on the contours of the cliff. She felt like a high wire walker, maintaining focus as she stepped slowly forwards.

Eventually, Debbie reached the waist high wall which edged the cycle path. She placed her hands and the warm stone edge and vaulted over it. From here- standing on the path- it was impossible to see the location of the mannequin, but the features of the rock below it were easy enough to identify. She walked to the wall nearest to the rock face and climbed up on to it. A passing cyclist gave Debbie a confused glance, but did not stop in their gliding journey along the beach path. Undeterred, Debbie began climbing up the sandstone slope. It was not particularly steep, but the smooth rounded face of the bluff made it difficult to ascend. Debbie cursed her curiosity and leaned forward to maintain her balance as she progressed, knowing if she tumbled backwards there would be nothing to grab on to.

When she was almost halfway up the bluff, Debbie saw something in a small crevice glinting in the bright sunlight. She reached her fingers into the shadowy fissure and made contact with something cold. She pulled her fingers out and discovered she had liberated a small jewel on a delicate gold chain. Some dreamy part of her mind suggested that the small item sparking in the sun so close to the ocean was like a piece of lost pirate treasure, but another more primitive part was starting to tell her to get out of there.

Ignoring her subconscious concerns, Debbie climbed higher. When she was around eighteen feet above the cycle path, she reached the area directly beneath the place where the mannequin appeared to be. She steadied her running shoes against the stony surface, and then used her hands to gripped the outcrop of rock and, with a grunt, she pulled herself up. It was in that moment that Debbie found herself confronted by the true nature of her discovery.

An angry cloud of flies buzzed around it in relentless swirls like black confetti., but even through the frenzied blur of the insects, Debbie could see the dead woman's bloated face and her opaque glassy eyes.

Despite her best efforts to remain calm, Debbie – who was frozen on her rocky perch- began to scream and scream.

## 24

Leighton sighed with relief and tapped his hands on the steering wheel in a small celebration. After getting lost on a woodland track, and subsequently having to drive in reverse for almost a quarter of a mile, he had eventually followed a serpentine road which wound along the edge of the sparkling lake. Having followed the winding route for twenty minutes, Leighton had been close to giving up when he glimpsed a square of white, just visible through the dark tangle of branches up ahead.

As his vehicle grew closer to the object, Leighton discovered he was looking at a weathered sign mounted on a squint wooden post. The faded writing on the scarred surface confirmed that *Lakehead Cabins* were half a mile further on. The round indentations peppering the sign suggested to Leighton that a couple of generations of locals had used the sign for target practice.

Leighton continued driving along the increasingly rough road, and then eventually glimpsed the angular shapes of buildings up ahead and the sparkling glint of water beyond them. Within a few moments, the road faded into a large open area of cabins which were set no more than ten or twelve feet from the edge of the lake. The place seemed almost part of the natural world, and Leighton could see why it would appeal to anyone hoping to escape the stresses of modernity.

After pulling his car into a parking area formed by logs around a rectangle of grey gravel, he got out of the car and closed the door. Breathing deeply the woodland air, Leighton savoured the dark aroma of rich soil and the sweet tang of pine and cedar. He then looked towards the lake and watched as a couple of large birds flew out over the lake then fluttered down to rest on the shimmering surface. The whole area felt soothing. It was the type of place where time no longer mattered, and Leighton suddenly understood the appeal of escaping to a location like this. There was no pollution here and no noise other than calming birdsong and the cheerful chirrup of bugs.

Leighton looked around at the snug cabins and found himself wondering if Heather would like to spend some time in a place like this rather than camping. She could even bring her books and combine the change of scene with her studies.

But now he had to push his ideas aside. He knew she was unhappy, and it ran deeper than simply wanting peace to study. While Leighton could still recall the softness of her tender kiss, the excitement in her voice as she shared her dreams and the warmth of her excited breath on his neck as he moved inside her; Heather now only ever talked about him as an irritation or unwelcome distraction – an anchor holding her back, expecting her to still be the person she clearly no longer wanted to be. As he listened to the sound of the crickets, part of Leighton suspected that privately Heather would probably would quite like to come back to somewhere like this…. but just not with him.

Pushing his sadness away, Leighton ambled across the carpet of rust coloured pine needles to the cluster of wooden cabins. There were four of them all angled in a row. Each cabin had its own single parking bay, marked out by white painted log. Each of them also had its own scorched brick barbecue and a weathered wooden picnic bench sitting by a small porch.

As he approached the cabins, Leighton realised that they all had a number painted in white on large boulders next to the parking areas. Leighton had no idea which one belonged to Nicholls, so he would just need to try his luck.

He was just about to step on to the porch of the nearest property when Leighton noticed a figure walking purposefully towards the cabins from the direction of the lake. The man-dressed in blue jeans and western style checked shirt- was walking through the trees and carrying a bundle of driftwood with such affection that, from his initial glance, Leighton had initially thought it may be an animal.

'Officer, can I help you?' he called to Leighton.

'Marc Nichols?'

'Sure, that's me.' The man walked over to where Leighton stood. His expression was one of mild concern.

'Mr Nichols, my name is Leighton Jones. I'd like to ask you a couple of questions.'

The man looked at the badge on Leighton's chest.

'You're an Oceanside cop?' Nichols asked as he set the sun bleached wood carefully down on the ground.

'Yes I am,' Leighton said.

Nichols nodded slowly. 'And you drove up all the way here from the coast?'

'Yes I did.'

'Okay then,' the man said calmly, 'That would suggest you must want to speak to me pretty bad- does that sound about right?'

'That's right.' Leighton watched as Nichol's shoulders slumped.

'Then if it's that serious, I guess you better come in and have some coffee – especially if you're planning to get back down to the coast tonight.'

'I am,' Leighton said, 'so that would be appreciated.'

Nichols led Leighton into the cabin which was neater and more comfortable than he had expected. Although rustic in terms of timber walls, the living area was stylish and featured a couple of couches draped in striped woollen blankets, a small coffee table and a number of large leaf plants. A sampler hung above the fireplace featured the words *shangri-la,* and featured an embroidered imaged of the cabin. Leighton wondered if it had been a gift from the neighbour he had spoken to. The lecturer invited Leighton to sit, whilst he entered the galley kitchen area to fix their coffee.

'Nice plants you have in here,' Leighton said.

'Yeah, I find them soothing. It brings the outdoors inside,' Nichols said as he returned with a tray on which were two steaming mugs. Setting the tray down, he nodded towards a large specimen over Leighton's shoulder. 'That one Is my favourite – Monstera Deliciosa.'

'Scary sounding name,' Leighton said as the lecturer handed him a mug.

'Don't be fooled by the name- it's a friendly big thing,' Nichols said as he eased himself on to one of the couches. 'Most people just call it a Swiss Cheese plant, but it's a favourite of mine. 'When I was a young boy back in Vermont, I used to like making dens in my garden – I'd hide amongst the plants there if was ever in trouble. I guess some habits just stick... even into adulthood.'

Leighton took a sip of steaming coffee then looked directly at the other man. 'Is that why you came out here, Mr Nicholls? Do you think you're in trouble that you need to hide from?' Leighton asked.

'Well, I presume that's why you're here?' Nicholls sighed. It was the sound of somebody who knew their fate and accepted it, but was in no hurry to get there.

Leighton decided to ease him into discussion with some simpler questions. 'So, how long have you worked at the university?'

'Three years. I was over at UCLA for four years before that.'

'Are there many students currently in your college classes?'

'It varies,' Nichols said with a small shrug of his shoulders. 'I mean I usually lecture to around two hundred students, but most of us also take smaller tutorial classes of around sixty.'

'So is a young woman named Kelly Coombs currently one of your students?'

'Ah, I suspected that was the reason for your visit.' Nicholls put down his mug and rubbed his hands together.

'Yeah? Well, why don't you go ahead and tell me about you and her?'

'Okay,' Nicholls sighed, 'she has been in my classes for around sixteen months.'

'Do you know her outside of college?'

'No, absolutely not!'

'I have a witness who has stated he saw you arguing with Kelly last Friday in the Santa Maria Hall parking lot. Is it possible he was mistaken?'

Nichols' eyes widened in horror.

'No, he wasn't mistaken.' Nichols looked at the floor, 'I wish to hell he was.'

'So what was going on?' Leighton asked.

'I was just speaking to her – she was a little upset so I suggested we talk in my car.'

'In your car?' Leighton asked.

'It was stupid, I know. I'm not surprised that she's reported it.'

'What was she upset about.'

'I told her to stay away from some guy.'

'Who?'

'A lecturer – Steve Brookes. The man likes to get a little too familiar with the students, if you know what I mean?'

Leighton nodded.

'Look, I'm generally not one to get involved in other people's business. I hadn't intended to say anything, but on Thursday afternoon he had been leaning on the water-cooler in the faculty lounge bragging loudly about how Kelly had the hots for him for him and how it wouldn't take him long to get into her pants.

When I couldn't stand listening to his disturbing shit any more, I walked out to the parking lot and sat in my car to have a smoke. That was when Kelly happened to be passing by. I called her over and asked her to get in. But only because I didn't want everyone hearing what we were talking about.' Nichols rubbed he hands together again.

'So what did you say to her?' Leighton asked.

'I told her to be careful and that she wouldn't be the first to have fallen for Brookes' charm offensive. I probably sounded like I was trying to be some kind of noble protector. What a jerk!'

'How did Kelly respond when you shared your concerns?'

Nichols chuckled. 'She told me to mind my own fucking business. I told her that I was only trying to look out for her. But she said that I was out of line and that if I spoke to her about Brookes again she would report me. Then she got out of the car.' He sighed. 'Can't really argue with that can you- forty-year-old guy telling an eighteen-year-old who she should or shouldn't be sleeping with? In any case the way she responded suggested to me that she's already a little enchanted by the professor. Maybe she thought I was speaking out of jealousy.'

'Were you?' Leighton held Nichols' gaze.

'Officer, I honestly say my concerns are purely for Kelly's welfare.'

'You sure about that?' Leighton pressed.

Nichols put down his coffee cup and crossed his legs. 'Do you mean did I want to have a relationship with her, is that it?'

'Well, it is possible. And you said, she maybe thought so too.'

'No, officer I do not want a relationship with Kelly. I'm gay. It's one of the reasons I moved from Cal State. My relationship with the faculty head – Alan Duke- broke down and I couldn't really work with him anymore.'

'Okay,' Leighton nodded. 'So, did you see Kelly again after your conversation on Thursday?'

'No, upon reflection I decided I'd embarrassed myself quite enough. My judgement was clearly affected, and I therefore spoke discretely to administration and asked if I could use up some of my holiday time. So here I am spending some quality time with William Faulkner and a family of local raccoons.'

'There are worse vacations,' Leighton said with a chuckle.

'Oh, there was something else,' Nichols added with a sudden tone of shame.

'What was that?' Leighton asked.

'I left a note for him.'

'Who?'

'Brookes,'

'What did it say? Did you mention Kelly?'

'Not explicitly. I just said that I knew what he was doing. I hoped that might be enough to get him to stop.'

'Look Mr Nichols,' Leighton shifted in his seat, wishing Alice Mead was with him to take care of this part. 'I'm going to be straight with you. Are you aware that Kelly's car was found?'

'Her car? What do you mean? Was there some kind of accident?'

'It was found dumped down at the lagoon in Oceanside. Nobody knows where she is. That's why I decided to take a drive up here.'

'Jesus, do you think she might have taken off because of what I said?'

'It's possible, but I doubt it.' Leighton said. 'If you are happy to give me a formal statement covering what you've just told me. I can head back down to the coast and hopefully find Kelly. You okay with that?'

'Of course,' I'm more than happy to make a statement or help in any way I can.'

Leighton drained the last of his coffee and set the mug down on the table. He then reached into his shirt pocket and took out his notebook. He hoped that Mr Nichols' information would bring him closer to discovering exactly what happened to Kelly Coombs, but he felt that things were become murkier rather than clearer.

## 25

On the second floor of the Alta Vista dormitories, Corey Troy stood outside the door of the apartment shared by Marie and Kelly. Speaking to the cop in town had made him feel as if he could be more than just an observer of events. Perhaps, for once, he could be like the heroic character featured in the novels he devoured so eagerly. There was only one problem, his actions in the past had been less than heroic. He knew that now.

After looking guiltily at his feet for a moment, he felt confident enough to knock on the blank wooden door. After a moment, it opened but only a fraction.

'Can I help you?' Lucy asked with a confused expression.

'Sorry to bother you. I was wondering if Kelly's around?'

'Sorry, who are you?'

'I'm Corey – I'm a lifeguard with Kelly over at the pool.'

'Oh, right.' Something shifted in Marie's eyes.

'So is she around?' Corey asked hopefully.

'No, she's not around just now.' Lucy said firmly.

'Do you know if anyone has seen her?'

'Look, I really can't tell you anything.' Marie moved to close the door.

'Well, if she's shows up, could you please tell her I called?'

'Sure,' Marie said and then closed the door. This was followed by the jangling sound of keys as the door was frantically locked.

Corey sighed and then reached into his back pocket and then ran his fingers over the smooth surface of Kelly's pass sat. He had momentarily considered giving the pass to her flatmate - maybe he could claim to have found it in the changing rooms, but he knew that she could easily hand over to the cops and then he would have to face some difficult questions. So instead of letting go of Kelly's pass, Corey looped the lanyard over his head and slipped the pass inside his t-shirt next to his skin.

# 26

Having taken a signed statement from Marc Nicholls, Leighton had only driven halfway along the forest track leading from the cabins to the interstate when his radio burst to life.

'This is a code one for Adam one-twenty-two. Pick up.'

Leighton reached for the handset and raised it to his mouth.

'Dispatch, this is Adam one-twenty-two

'Go ahead,' he said, but for a moment there was nothing by silence. Leighton glanced down at the radio and took his foot of the gas.

'Officer Jones we have been trying to reach you with a request that you find a telephone and contact Officer Mead ASAP.'

'Thanks dispatch will do, out.'

Leighton pulled his car into the forecourt of a Shell gas station just outside of Riverside and stepped out in the hot, fumy air. He walked over to a scuffed payphone mounted on the side of the building. After rummaging in his trouser pocket for a couple of quarters, Leighton dialled the phone number of the traffic desk. It was answered by the familiar voice of another traffic officer.

'Hey Tom, it's Leighton Jones. Is Alice around?'

'Sure, she was just about to leave. Hang on I'll see if I can catch her at the lockers.'

'Thanks, buddy.'

There followed a few minutes of relative silence punctuated by the sound of a telephone ringing or a murmur of conversation. Suddenly there was a clacking noise as the phone was picked up.

'Hey Rookie! You called just in time – I was just about to jump on the saddle.'

'So I heard. How are things down there?'

'Pretty interesting, where are you?'

'At a gas station in Moreno Valley Just heading back from Big Bear Lake. What's up?'

'A call just came in this afternoon. They just found another body down at Carlsbad beach. Jim Daniels and his team are there right now. '

'Shit! Was the body in another car?'

'No, it was sprawled halfway down the bluff. But from the initial details buzzing around the station, it sounds like she had a driving license in her back pocket that confirms she's our girl from the lagoon. What about your lead, did you manage to locate him?'

'Yeah, the guy is living up in one of the cabins on the lakeside, but he's clean. Apparently, the reason he was seen fighting with Kelly was because he was trying to warn her about another creepy college lecturer.'

'Wow, two creepy professors for the price of one,' Alice said with a laugh.

'No, just one of them. It seems like Nichols was just trying to do the right thing.'

'Well, did you get a name of this *one* creepy guy?'

'Yeah – Steve Brookes. He's a teacher in the Humanities faculty, and it sounds like he likes to get a little too close to the students. I have a contact over at the college administration who can probably confirm his home address if we can't lift it off the system.'

'Good work, Rookie! You get your ass back here and first thing tomorrow we can pass this on to Daniels and Homicide.'

'I'm only an hour away; I might be back in time to catch him tonight- well, hopefully'

'Sure, you sound tired. Everything else okay?'

'Yeah, of course. I'm good, it's just been a long drive,' Leighton lied.'

'That's called road fatigue – it comes with working traffic. You're just lucky that I take the wheel most of the time to save your soft ass.'

'You spend time thinking about my soft ass, officer? I'm not sure that's appropriate – especially at your advanced age.'

'Bite me, Rookie. If I'm not still hanging around here, I'll see you in the morning,' Alice said and then hung up.

## 27

The sky was fading to orange as Leighton drove into the parking lot of Oceanside Police Station. Turning into one of the parking bays assigned to Traffic cruisers, he noticed that Alice's silver bicycle was already chained to the sign marked 'staff parking only'. He suspected that she may have wanted to sound out Jim Daniels before going to the chief.

Leighton had only just crossed the parking lot, when Alice stormed out of the building. She was shaking her head had a frown like a v-shaped cut in her forehead.

'What's up?' Leighton asked as Alice approached him.

'Honestly, Rookie, you're not going to believe this shit.' Alice put her hands on her hips- a move Leighton had only ever seen her do when she was particularly irritated. 'I just spoke with Jim Daniels – laid it all out nice and clear for him like a picnic on a fuckin' blanket– two cars, two young female victims, both dead in similar circumstances with a suspect linking them both.

'I take he didn't share our take on things?' Leighton asked, but suspected her already knew the answer.

'Damn right. He said that he could see how it might look like a little suspicious but Homicide isn't interested in taking either case any further.'

'What do you mean – is the investigation being passed to Vice?'

'No,' Alice shook her head. 'Daniels and the captain have decided it's a matter of case closed- period. Apparently, the evidence in both cases could support the theory that the two deaths were both suicides – nothing more.'

'What?'

'He told me they fast-tracked the autopsy on Kelly Coombs this afternoon and the chief is preparing to sign off on the paperwork already. They are *anticipating* that the autopsies on both girls will conclude both are inconclusive because they couldn't definitively point to the involvement of anyone else.'

'What the he'll does 'anticipating' mean?'

'It means they have decided the outcome and now want to make the evidence fit.'

'How the hell could somebody else not be involved in the deaths?'

'Yep- that's what I asked. Apparently, the trauma to both girls could be easily explained as self- inflicted. The ME said the girl at Windmill lake's superficial injuries, prior to drowning could've come from her car crashing into the water at speed, and Kelly Coomb's fatal head trauma from a fall from the boulevard on to the rocks.'

'Yeah, but it could also indicate the involvement of an attacker. Jeez. 'How do they explain the car being in the lagoon and the driver being found half a mile away on a fucking cliff?'

'Daniels has a theory that Kelly Coombs drove into the lake- possibly intentionally, but she then got out of the vehicle, staggered back up on the boulevard, found the highest point and threw herself or fell over it.'

'That's such bullshit!'

'Yep, why the fuck would somebody take a nosedive off a cliff their preferred way to end their life?'

'So what's going on? Why the shift in focus?'

'Apparently drug related deaths are the current priority for all law enforcement across the USA, so looking into whatever happened to those two girls won't get the Chief an invite to the Whitehouse.'

'Well, hopefully their families of the victims won't accept this whitewash.'

'I doubt any family members will be showing up to kick up a stink,' Alice said with a sigh.

'What do you mean?'

'Apparently, the girl whose body we saw at Windmill Lake – one Sarah Levin- had been in a ward of the state in a care home in San Bernardino since her mom went for a ten-year stretch in Chino prison on serious drugs charges. The girl ran away aged fifteen and nobody went looking for her. The first record of her in Oceanside is from three years ago. Apparently Sarah had a waitressing job up until a couple of weeks ago?'

'So, how did she pay for the car on coffee shop wages?'

'It was rented, and there was a fully packed holdall on the back seat- pretty much everything she owned stuffed in one bag. Anyway, Daniels' theory is that after losing her job, the girl was probably thinking of driving back to Seattle – or maybe just moving on again.'

'So why take her own life? She packed a goddam bag – hardly the actions of someone about to end their life!'

'Exactly. You can see why I'm not buying it, and I'm sure you're not either.'

Leighton shook his head. 'This stinks. What about Kelly Coombs, she had a job and she was in college. No-one I spoke to mentioned her being in any way suicidal or depressed – and even if both girls were, why wouldn't she reach out to the grandparent back home?'

'I don't know about Kelly's family but the Levin girl's landlord said she was estranged from her family in Oregon, they'll say the same about Kelly, put it alongside some bullshit claim of college pressure to make the idea of suicide stick.'

Leighton ran his hand through his hair. 'This is totally messed up. I can't believe they're calling two matching deaths in the same week fucking suicides.'

'The whole thing's bullshit, Rookie. It's just political. The deaths of those two young woman are being swept under the rug so we can get a pat on the back and a shiny badge from Nancy fucking Reagan.'

'What can we do about it?' Leighton asked.

Alice took Leighton by the arm and led him away from the station building to a quiet area of the parking lot. She then looked at him and raised her eyebrows.

'Why did you become a cop, Leighton?'

'Whoa, if you're using my Sunday name, this must be serious.'

'I mean it,' Alice persisted, 'Why did you choose this shit-show as your circus of choice?'

'To help people – maybe make a difference I guess,' Leighton said with a shrug.

'Me too,' Alice said with a nod. 'So what harm would there be if we simply carried on looking into the case? We could do that couldn't we?'

'But I thought the captain said we should drop it,' Leighton said with a shrug.

'If the captain told you to jump in front of a speeding bus would you do it?'

'I guess not,' Leighton conceded.

'Look Rookie, as you get older you'll realise that having a couple more stripes on your sleeve doesn't mean you're a better cop; it just means you kissed the right butts and repeated whatever bullshit comes out of City Hall. Now, I'm not saying there's anything wrong with that – if you want the big bucks or perhaps the sense of power – but none of that makes you a better cop.'

'Well that explains why you never made Captain,' Leighton said with a smile.

'Yeah, well who the hell would want to sit in a pokey little office scratching their ass all day anyway.'

'So, where do we begin?' Leighton asked.

'We are on the early shift tomorrow. I reckon if we shift our butts and complete the traffic checks for this morning, we can take this afternoon to dig a little deeper into the case.'

'Remember I'm just a traffic cop,' Leighton said with a nervous laugh. 'I have a limited skill set.'

'You're a good cop and that's all that matters.'

'I hope you're right.'

'I usually am,' Alice said with a chuckle, 'I'll do a bit of sniffing around find out what I can about the girl from Windmill Lake – where she lived, where she worked; you can keep an eye on this creepy guy Brookes.'

'Sure,' Leighton nodded.

'And it's best you take your own car and get out of uniform – travel under the radar. '

# 28

Dressed in faded jeans and grey t-shirt, and wearing a San Diego Padres baseball cap, Leighton. entered the coffee shop which was located among a cluster of other businesses on Old Grove Road. The area comprised a large L-shape of hacienda style buildings, and a long glass-fronted Ralph's grocery store.

Inside the coffee shop, the warm aroma of coffee and vanilla hung in the hazy air, and a handful of customers were sprinkled around the few tables. A couple of teenage girls in fluorescent orange t-shirts were sitting together, sipping on matching glasses of lurid pink milkshakes whilst giggling at the problem page of a magazine, an older man in a white pant suit was sitting by the door reading a paperback and occasionally fanning himself with it. A younger guy in a business suit was fiddling with a yellow Walkman, however the person Leighton was looking for was sitting alone in the corner, nursing a coffee and looking out on the street.

After spending the morning running random DUI stops – which also included a freshly mandated drug search- on the boulevard and then returning to the station to fill in the requisite paperwork, Leighton had lifted Brookes' car details from the DMV records. His file had confirmed his current home in Cardiff Bay Drive as well as a previous address in over in Salton City. After making a note of these details, Leighton had taken a drive over to the USD campus where he spent almost an hour locating it the in faculty parking lot.

Eventually, Leighton had parked within viewing distance, and then entered the Literature building. His casual attire- and relative youth- made it easy for Leighton to blend into the tide of students. Thankfully, the schedules of weekly lectures and associated staff were posted on typed notices, which were thumb-tacked to the various felt display boards throughout the building. Leighton had stood in front of one and noted the timings of Brookes' lectures. There were three of them —marked as SBL2 — the last one finishing at 3.50pm.

That meant Leighton had a couple of hours to wait until Brookes was due to leave.

After grabbing a club sandwich wrapped in wax paper and a coffee from a bustling commons diner in the basement of the building, Leighton had carried his lunch outside, where he sat on the grass and placed the items on the neatly mowed lawn. He then pulled his note-pad from his back pocket and flipped it open. He sat it beside the coffee and picked up his sandwich. Sitting amongst the other students who were scattered around the neat lawns, Leighton could easily have been mistaken for a post-graduate student looking over lecture notes.

As he glanced around, Leighton thought that perhaps somewhere like this – in the warm sunshine and with other people- would a healthier place for Heather to study, rather than being holed up in their cramped, gloomy apartment. However, he knew she would say that she couldn't study with other people around – or perhaps just him.

As he ate in the warm sunshine, Leighton carefully poured over the details of the crimes.

It was easier than thinking about what was wrong at home.


He had returned to his car ten minutes before Brookes was due to finish his final lecture of the day. Leighton had hoped the guy didn't have any faculty meetings to attend, or he could be waiting a while. Luckily, Steve Brookes had appeared fairly quickly and climbed into his red Lancia.

Leighton had carefully tailed him out of the bustling campus, and noted how Brookes had slowed down to politely allow any female students wearing shorts to cross in front of his car. Leighton didn't think this gesture was in any way altruistic.

After leaving the familiarity of the college campus, Brookes had driven on to the clamorous Interstate 15 which headed back towards Oceanside. Leighton managed to merge into the surging traffic and follow him at safe distance. For most of the trip, he used a large white Fed Ex truck as a buffer between Brooke's car and his own.

There was only one scary moment as they were both passing by Black Mountain, when Brooke's car suddenly slowed down. Leighton, who was in an adjacent lane, saw the brake lights glare up ahead and was forced to take his foot off the gas or risk being seen.

Almost immediately the air was filled with an angry blare of horns from behind Leighton's vehicle. He glanced in his rear view mirror to discover that a previously unseen bus was suddenly dangerously close to him. His small car shuddered as the raging vehicle pulled out and rumbled on by.

Leighton exhaled a long breath. Luckily, he had remained far enough back from Brookes' car that it was unlikely that he would have been visible. Despite that, the brush with the bus had left him rattled. He was all too familiar with the damage done to cars and drivers on California's roads.

After he had left the interstate, Leighton had followed Brooke on Highway 76 until he reached Old Grove Road. Keeping several cars between them, Leighton had followed Brooke's Lancia as it pulled into the tree lined parking lot of a large grocery store. The red roofed store shared the parking lot with a cluster of other single storey outlets – Unfortunately, the place was crammed full of cars. Apparently, this was prime time for families coming back from the school pick up to stop off for dinner supplies. Leighton had watched the lecturer's car circle the lot before it finally vanished behind a chilled foods delivery truck which was parked outside an adjacent Pizza Hut. Leighton waited, watching the truck, but the Lancia did not re-emerge on the other side.

'Shit!' Leighton pulled his car into an available parking bay. After, climbing out of the vehicle, he jogged through the lanes of parked cars until he reached the delivery truck. As he hurried around the side of it, Leighton discovered that the truck's position had blocked his view of an alleyway leading to the rear of the outlets. If this provided an exit back on to the freeway, Brookes could be miles away.

Leighton glanced around and then wandered into the alley. It led to another smaller parking lot with a wall-mounted sign stating that is was for staff use only. Leighton breathed a sigh of relief when he noticed the Lancia was parked in one of the bays, but there was, however, no sign of Brookes. Hurrying back around to the front of the building, Leighton looked all around but he still couldn't see any sign of the lecturer among the people drifting in and out of the various outlets. Then as he scanned the glass windows of the various shops and eateries, Leighton noticed Brookes sitting close to the window of a small coffee shop.

Leighton eased himself on to a tall wooden stool at the long coffee counter, and picked up a laminated menu which featured colourful drawings of various items. He dragged one finger down the list of hot drinks and frowned as if concentrating on making a selection – he wasn't. Instead, Leighton was using a long mirror behind the coffee counter to observe Brookes.

Leighton had only been sitting at the counter for a moment when a teenage waitress wearing a burgundy apron came over to serve him.

'Hi there,' she said with a smile, 'I'm Kirsty, welcome to The Gingerbread House, what can I get for you?'

'Just a black coffee please,' Leighton said, 'In a take-out cup if possible.'

'No problem, sir that'll one-eighty.'

Leighton paid for his coffee and told the waitress to keep the change. Whilst she used a large gurgling machine to fill steaming cup, he shifted to ensure he could see Brooke's reflection.

'Thanks,' Leighton said as the waitress set his cup down.

'You're welcome,' she said cheerfully, 'can I get you anything else?'

'Kirsty, do you see the guy sitting behind me in the corner?'

The girl momentarily stood on her tip toes to look over Leighton's shoulder to where Steve Brooke was sipping his frothy coffee and gazing absently out of the window.

'Yeah, sure I do.' The girl nodded but appeared a little puzzled by the question.

'Hey It's okay Kirsty,' Leighton said reassuringly, 'I'm a cop.' He turned over his right hand to give the girl a glimpse of the badge he had been concealing pressed flat on the counter. 'I'm only asking because he looks a little like somebody who has been breaking into cars in the area. I just want to ask a couple of questions without spooking the guy. In any case, I'm probably wrong. Is that okay?' he asked.

'The girl nodded and appeared more relaxed. She picked up a cloth and began wiping down the counter. 'What do you want to know?'

'How often does he come in here?' Leighton asked.

'I'd say every other day. I only work three afternoons per week after school, but he's usually here. Pretty much always sitting in the same seat too.'

'You sure about that?' Leighton asked

'Yeah,' the girl said as she rinsed out the cloth in a sink beneath the counter. 'He sits in that corner and orders a large cappuccino – sometimes two. His name is Steve.'

'You know his name?'

'Yeah. He's really friendly and likes to chat to us all. I mean, sometimes it's a little annoying because we have tables to clear or other customers to serve, and he wants to talk about real deep stuff. That's why I don't really think he's the guy you're looking for.'

'You don't- how come?''

'Steve is a college professor, so he wouldn't need to break into cars or anything like that.'

No,' Leighton said, 'I guess not.'

He took a sip of coffee. 'How do you know that he's a professor.'

Everyone here knows that. He even offers to tutor any of the girls who need extra help with school or college in return for coffees and cupcakes?'

'Wow,' Leighton said, 'that's pretty generous.'

'I know right,' Kirsty said.

'Anyone take him up on the offer?'

'Well, not me. I was never that into school.'

'Me neither,' Leighton said with a chuckle.

'But I think maybe Sarah did. I'm not sure. She hasn't been around for a while.'

'No?'

'Yeah,' Kirsty dropped her voice to a whisper. 'I think she was maybe fired by the boss.'

'Well, I guess you're right- he's clearly not the guy I thought he was. My mistake. Thanks for talking with me.'

Leighton stood up, picked up his coffee and then walked to the door.

'Anytime,' Kirsty said as she wiped at a persistent stain on the counter.

Stepping into the sunshine, Leighton walked swiftly around the block to where his car was parked. After climbing inside, he placed his coffee cup in the holder between the seats, and then removed his cap. He started the car and drove back around the corner, passing the coffee shop before pulling into the nearby parking lot of Ralph's. He switched off the engine. The car's position among the others was not obvious and allowed Leighton a clear view of Steve Brookes.

Leighton watched, him for just over an hour. During that time, Brooke ordered a second coffee, and read the LA Times- occasionally stopping to chat with any passing waitress.

Eventually, he left and Leighton followed him to his home address on the north side of the city. There was nothing to see after Brookes had entered the family home, but Leighton remained parked up a short distance away.

On the way back to the station, Leighton pulled his car over at a payphone on Mission Avenue. He picked up the handset and called home. As the phone rang, Leighton could imagine the noise echoing through his home at the other end. Heather could be sitting on the floor surrounded by books, or she may not be at home at all. He let the phone ring another five times and then gave up. He wondered if Heather had been there but just let ring.

Eventually, Leighton concluded there was no point in trying again. He sighed and then dialled Alice's number.

'Hello, this is Alice Mead.'

'Alice it's me.'

'Hey Rookie, what's the news?'

'Well I've got a fair bit.'

'You wanna grab a coffee and fill me in.'

'Sure.'

'Where are you just now?'

'Just off Mission Avenue, south side.'

'Okay head down to Rubies on the pier. I'll be there in ten.'

'If I get there before you, what do you want?'

'Surprise me,' Alice said and hung up.

## 29

Alice and Leighton were sitting at an outdoor table on Oceanside Pier. It was a warm evening, and people were wandering by, eating ice-cream and enjoying the view of the black clad surfers riding the tumbling waves.

On the table in front of the officers were two half empty coffee cups and the crumbs left behind from two slices of apple pie.

'Okay Rookie, so now that you're fed and watered, what have we got to go on?'

Leighton pulled his black notepad from his chest pocket and flipped it open.

'Two dead girls, similar age, both Caucasian, similar build, and both connected to two cars that were found abandoned in similar circumstances.'

'Okay,' Alice nodded.

'And,' Leighton emphasised this word, 'it seems that both of the deceased were involved with the same guy.'

'Is that confirmed?'

'Well, we it's a matter of public record that Kelly was in his college class. As for Sarah, I followed him out of college this afternoon.'

'To where?'

'Ralph's.'

'The grocery store?'

'Yeah, well to a coffee shop located pretty much next to it. According to a waitress I spoke to, our guy is a regular, and likes to get all up close and personal with the girls working there. Even without the issue of potential links to the sunken vehicles this would be ringing some alarm bells, but when you cross reference his behaviour with the dead girl the whole thing stinks.'

'It sure does,' Alice nodded, 'but, that'll never fly on its own. Even some squeaky clean lawyer straight out of college could rip it apart. '

'Yeah, well that would be their mistake. Look, there's something else.'

'Hit me with it,' Alice said.

'Just after I tailed Brookes back along Douglas Drive and he pulled into Cardiff Bay Drive that I remembered something.'

'Remembered what?'

'Last fall a teenage girl called Amy-Lee Hollander was found dead at one of those properties in that street. '

'Jeez, I remember too. Daniels said it was a tough one. The kid was drunk, right?'

'Yeah- supposedly. But here's the thing – she was found face down in the backyard pool of a property numbered 1618.'

'Practically next door to your sleaze-ball lecturer.'

'Exactly.'

'Holy shit. I mean that's more than a fucking coincidence, right?'

'To you and I, yes; to Jim Daniels, possibly not.'

'So what do we do?' Alice asked- almost to herself.

'We could drop it?' Leighton suggested. 'Get back to traffic management and driver awareness classes, do our day jobs.'

'No way, we can't let this go!'

'But like you said, we've got nothing solid here so it makes you wonder if there's any point throwing any more energy at it.'

'Rookie, those two girls have nobody fighting for them. If you're doing the right thing, you can't let assholes and difficulties get in your way.'

'I know,' Leighton said with a shrug, 'but, I guess sometimes life is shit. It's not like we can fix everything for the entire population of Oceanside! Not everyone has somebody in their corner.'

'You finished?' Alice shot him a look that indicated he damn well should be.

'Yeah, I guess,' Leighton sighed. 'Look, I'm sorry Alice. I'm just tired. I know these girls deserve better.'

Alice nodded and picked up her coffee cup. 'Can I ask you something – and you can tell me to back off?'

'Sure,' Leighton shrugged.

'How are things at home?'

'Oh, come on, that's not fair!' Leighton tilted his head back. 'I thought you were going to ask me about the case.'

'Some things are more important.' Alice held Leighton's gaze.

Leighton sighed. 'Look, things aren't great, I get it, but Heather and I can work things out.'

'Okay, Leighton. I hope you do.'

'Thanks.'

'But I know from experience how it feels to be struggling to keep going in a relationship that's going nowhere. It can sometimes be a real lonely place to be. I don't think I ever felt so alone as when my marriage was drifting apart.'

'But you live alone here now,' Leighton said, 'isn't that pretty much the same?'

'No, definitely not.' Alice smiled ruefully. 'The loneliness of two people living together but feeling separate is a hell of a lot worse than living on your own.'

'Because now it's your choice.' Leighton said softly.

'Exactly. So if things at your place get any more difficult-'

'They won't.'

Leighton turned his head to look at the long churning waves.

'If they somehow do,' Alice continued, 'I want you to know that there's a spare room at mine.'

'Thanks Alice, but I can honestly make it work. Heather is just going through a rough patch. I guess everyone gets fed up with their lives at some point. It can't be easy being married to a cop.'

'No, it certainly wasn't for my ex. But just like you said yourself not everything can be fixed.'

'Yeah, but some things can be. We can be. I'll figure it out – honestly.'

'What is it that seems to be the issue between you?'

'I don't know – I guess she wants to study and get ahead, and she thinks I'm holding her back?'

'Are you?'

'Hell no! I want her to be happy. I want her to find something that she loves.'

'Does Heather know that – have you actually told her?'

'Yeah. I guess.'

'Well, maybe you should remind her, but regardless, the offer stands,' Alice said resolutely.

'Okay,' Leighton said reluctantly.

'Right,' Alice nodded, 'back to the case. I got on to UCSD records office. Asked if Kelly Coombs had reported any issues with her professors.'

'Had she?' Leighton asked.

'No,' Alice said as she checked over her shoulder, 'but she had submitted two reports of harassment to administration.'

Leighton frowned. 'If she wasn't getting bothered by any lecturers, who was harassing her?'

'Apparently it was another student.'

'What?' Leighton felt knocked off balance. 'Did you get a name?'

'I sure did,' Alice said with a wry smile, 'Corey Troy- a Caucasian male aged nineteen.'

'Holy shit!'

'You know him?'

'Yeah, that's the kid who came to me to report on Marc Nicholls.'

'Wow! Do you reckon he could have been pestering the girl and was happy to shift focus on to some teacher out of jealousy?'

'Maybe. What does the report say he did?'

'The report only states harassment.'

'Was there are record of an action taken?'

'Yeah, he the records states that he received a verbal warning from the head of student services.'

'When was all of this?'

'Back at the start of the semester.'

'What do you reckon?' Leighton felt out of his depth and felt rattled by the possibility that he might have shared his car with a killer.'

'Well, I pulled his address off the system. I was thinking of going to speak to him in the morning.'

'You think he's involved- working with Brookes?'

'I don't know. I just reckon we need to stay open to all possibilities.'

'So what do you want me to do? I can't just follow Brookes around. If he did it, there must be evidence we could find.'

'I agree, but I also know from my days in vice that sometimes tailing a person is the best way to get the evidence. If Brookes did kill those girls he will screw up – and if you are on his tail, you'll catch him screwing up.'

Leighton nodded.

'Look, Rookie, I know you've not had the easiest run recently.'

'I'm not the only one. Everybody has their shit to deal with.'

'Yeah, but you've got to build some time in to decompress. Look, how about after this thing is all finished we come down here and order a couple of strawberry ice cream sundaes, and then head to the Rooster and get hammered.

'Is that whilst you're still on duty?'

'What they gonna do, fire me?'

'Well, either way, it's something to look forward to,' Leighton said with a grin.

# 30

It was a little after eleven by the time Leighton arrived home. He was glad to discover that Heather was still awake. During the drive from Alice's home to his own, Leighton had stared solemnly ahead and mentally rehearsed different ways in which he could tell Heather that he was supportive – that he did want her to succeed.

It was the truth.

He knew that she was smarter than him, but ever since high school, Heather had been disinterested in committing to any career plan. The summer after leaving school, Leighton had followed his father and taken a job in the Kaiser Steel Mill, the work was hot and hard, but he knew that it was only ever a stepping stone to his real ambition of joining the military. Heather, however had never understood Leighton's drive to settle into a specific career had said that she found the idea of sticking to the same job every day quite depressing. This lack of direction had meant that any jobs Heather took on were poorly paid, and often involved serving food or drink to the public. Yet, over the years of pulling frothy beers down town, she grew unhappy with the lack of challenge and began to look into local college courses. Eventually- and still with a degree of reluctance- she signed up for a three year course in Kindergarten teaching.

When he entered the small hallway, Leighton could hear the sound of Heather brushing her teeth coming from behind the closed door of the tiny bathroom. Eventually, he heard the sound of running water stop, the door clicked open and then Heather appeared in the bedroom doorway.

'Hi,' Leighton said. 'sorry I'm so late.

'Where were you – the bar?'

'No, I tried calling earlier to let you know my plans. I was just talking with Alice.'

'What a surprise,' Heather said as she pushed by Leighton.

'What's that supposed to mean?'

Heather's expression darkened. 'Nothing,' she said sullenly.

'No come on, you put it out there. What's the big issue?' Leighton folded his arms.

'Well, it just seems like every time that old woman snaps her fingers you go running to her?'

'Christ, I don't believe this! Are you jealous of Alice?'

Heather looked at him with an expression bordering on pity. 'No, Leighton I'm not jealous of her.'

'So what's your problem? If I'm at home, you look pissed at me; if I am out, you complain and looked pissed when I get home. Jeez, I can't do anything right. I honestly feel like you just don't want me to be here anymore.'

Heather looked at him for a moment, and moved her lips momentarily as if to speak, but then she simply went into the bedroom and quietly closed the door. Her silence was more hurtful than any words could have been.

Leighton padded through to the small laundry room where he kept his uniform. It was a cramped windowless space which contained little more than a washing machine, shelves of detergent and a propped up striped ironing board. Thankfully, Heather didn't want Leighton's work clothes hanging in the bedroom wardrobe — she said they stank of the highway, even after they had been laundered- so his shirts and trousers were consigned to two single hangers on a brass hook fastened to the laundry room wall. Tonight this arrangement was a good thing for

Leighton. It meant he was able to organise clean clothes for the morning without confronting Heather again.

Having stripped down to his white boxer shorts, Leighton bundled his shirt and trousers into the washing machine, poured in some detergent, and switched it on. He then pulled out the ironing board, and plugged the cheap plastic iron into a wall socket.

After carefully pressing his uniform, Leighton hung the warm trousers and shirt on a spare wire hanger and then he put the iron and board away. When his preparation for the day ahead was complete, reached up to the shelf above the washing machine, and selected a grey blanket, which he carried through to the small dark living room. The air was warm and stifling, but rather than switch on the air-conditioning, Leighton threw the blanket on the couch and then walked over to the window. He gripped the handle, turned it and then slid the window open a couple of inches. The sound of traffic and muted music drifted inside like a welcome ghost. Leighton offered a sad smile, life in the city, it seemed, continued as normal.

Leighton walked back to the couch and lay down. The couch was old and beat up but would serve as a decent alternative to the floor.

It took a while for sleep to come, and before it finally did, Leighton had decided that he would speak to Alice in the morning to ask if he could stay at her place- at least for a couple of days.

For the second time, in a week Leighton found himself sleeping alone in the small apartment he shared with Heather, and he knew that wasn't good.

# 31

At 7.40 am, the last remnants of mist were still to burn off, but the area of sky directly above Oceanside was blue and cloudless. Leighton had awoken early with a stiff neck. He had got dressed in his uniform and then left the silent apartment earlier than usual. If Heather had been awake, she hadn't wanted her husband to know it, but the victory was a pointless one; Leighton was in no hurry to speak to her either. He wouldn't even know what to say.

However, before her left his apartment, Leighton made a hushed phone call to Westmorland Police Department. It was easier to call from home than risk being overheard at the station. He left a message asking if they could confirm any instances of missing or murdered local women in recent years. It was long shot, but if Brookes was killing in his current local area, perhaps he had done it at his previous address too.

As Leighton drove the two miles from his apartment to the police station on Mission Avenue, he felt as if he was standing on the edge of some crumbling precipice. He had been with Heather for most of his adult life and her presence had always seemed like a comforting certainty. Now everything seemed suddenly fragile, and his dream of a future together was dissolving.

But despite his youth, Leighton also had a quiet sense of dignity, and he would rather move out than creep around his home, whilst Heather appeared as if she couldn't bear to look at him. He could handle not feeling loved, but he couldn't handle feeling unwanted.

He thought that perhaps if he and Alice took a drive over to the university together, the conversation would naturally shift to his home-life again and this time – as embarrassing as it would be- he could ask if he could move in to her place for a couple of nights.

At least he had that as an option. Maybe that would give them enough space to figure things out.

Leighton crossed the sunlit parking lot and entered the station locker room. As his eyes adjusted from the morning brightness to the relative gloom, he was initially unsure of who the figure sitting on one of the wooden benches was. At first, he assumed the other individual was simply another officer preparing for the day. He suddenly realised that the hunched figure staring down at its feet was actually the captain.

'Morning sir,' Leighton nodded, 'We don't often we see you down here in the locker area.'

'No, I guess you don't.' The captain stood up. 'Listen officer, can I speak to you for a moment?'

'Sure,' Leighton shrugged.

'In my office.' The captain gestured with is head towards the doorway leading out of the locker room.

'Of course,' Leighton replied quickly, but the captain had already walked away towards the management area of the building.

As both officers passed by the dispatch room the two female officers, inside who had been talking excitedly in hushed voices, glanced at the doorway and fell strangely silent.

'Sir, can I ask if I am I in some kind of trouble?' Leighton said as he walked into the office, which smelled of coffee and stale cigar smoke.

The captain remained standing but leaned back on his wooden desk and began to massage the back of his neck with one hand. His eyes narrowed.

'No, officer you're not in any trouble – at least not in the way you mean. Close the door will you.'

Leighton did as he was told and then turned around to face his superior.

'Look,' the captain said with a sigh, 'Leighton, there's no easy way to say this.'

'To say what?' Leighton felt his stomach suddenly tighten.

'Your partner, Alice Mead, was involved in a road traffic accident this morning- she was hit by a truck. Apparently, she was cycling into work on the boulevard when it knocked her off her bike. We don't know exactly what caused it but-'

Leighton felt like he had been punched in the gut. He had anticipated many things but not this. He was aware the captain was speaking but he couldn't process any of it.

'Where is she?' he asked.

'Over in Tri City Medical Centre, but at this stage we-'

'I'd like to see her,' Leighton said abruptly.

'Sure, okay,' the captain nodded. 'But you probably want to prepare yourself. Donna DeLuca from of our emergency team called me personally to say that Alice was hurt pretty bad.'

'Yeah, but you know Alice,' Leighton said with a forced smile, 'she's a real fighter. I'll just bring her flowers and a bottle of rum. Maybe some-'

'Leighton,' the captain looked suddenly defeated, 'there's a real possibility she might not make it through this.'

Leighton paused for a moment as a flicker of panic crossed his face, but it was quickly replaced with an expression of hope. 'We'll see.' Leighton said, but his mind was eleven miles away.

'Okay,' you get over to the hospital and see how she's holding up. Take as much time as you need,' the captain said.

## 32

Steve Brookes was wearing a blue denim shirt and pair of carefully placed wayfarer sunglasses on the top of his head as he sat at a large wooden table in a corner of the university's Coley library. The morning sun was bright and illuminated the interior of the building in shafts of light. Spread on the table in front of Brookes were a number of books and a large legal pad containing some hand written notes. He was holding a silver coloured ballpoint pen in his right hand, whilst using his cocked thumb to absently click the button on top of it.

The long tables nearby were populated by a number of students, most of them engaged in quiet research.

To an outside observer, Brookes may simply have appeared to be an eager lecturer preparing notes for his next college class, but that wasn't quite right. He was preparing, but not for any class. Brookes was adding to his list of his current interesting *specimens*.

This included any young women who Brookes felt matched his specific type and were therefore likely to become potential projects. Brookes was practically fizzing with energy as he carefully wrote down the names and details of each person. Three names at the top of the list had been scored out: Amy Lee Hollister, Sarah Levin, Kelly Coombs. These had been his past conquests, and each of them evoked a certain sadness in Steve – not so much for the fate of the young woman as for himself. He would never again enjoy the thrill of watching from distance, then getting close to each of them, and using his charm to possess them and ultimately have them. It was a primal activity, which made him feel alive.

After the names of the three previous girls was that of another – not yet scored out. Leona Carlson. She was in Steve's second year tutorial group, and was petite and blonde with an athletic physique. When Brookes had overheard her talking to her friends about cheerleader practice, he had taken a sudden interest in the college football team. He had bought an expensive pair of binoculars and had gone over to sit in the bleachers and apparently watch a couple of games, but he was only ever focussed on Leona. And even though he could watch her skip and dance around the football field, Steve was still not satisfied. The distance seemed too far. He preferred experiencing Leona up close. She always came to class wearing tennis shorts and a loose fitting shirt that left little to the imagination. Brookes knew that she chose to dress like that especially for him. But more than how she looked, Brookes liked how Leona smelled. Her fragrance was a sweet perfume that reminded the lecturer of the warm cotton candy he had devoured as a kid. He had even asked Leona what the perfume was called, and when she said it was called Lou Lou, he had written it down. On the way home that afternoon, he had stopped off at the mall that afternoon and bought a small crystal shaped bottle. But now owning the aroma and the image of

Leona in his mind, was still not enough for Steve Brookes. It was time to take the relationship to the next level.

33

Leighton entered the vast white foyer of the Medical Centre. The building featured a great deal of glass and white walls. To Leighton it had always seemed similar to an airport. Both places shared the prospect of new arrivals and departures. Crossing the glossy floor,

Leighton was self-consciously carrying a white fluffy toy cat and a bouquet of bright yellow flowers. He glanced around at the various people criss-crossing the tiled floor, and then eventually located the reception. Leighton took a deep breath and then cautiously approached the desk where a male receptionist smiled revealing unnaturally white teeth.

'Good afternoon, officer,' he said confidently, 'welcome to Tri County, I'm Graham, how can I help you?'

'I'm here to visit a patient. Her name is Alice Mead. I understand she was brought in this morning?'

'Uh huh.' Graham nodded, 'and can you tell me the patient's date of birth?'

'No,' Leighton said, 'I'm sorry I don't know Alice's date of birth. I mean I know it's in June.'

'Are you a member of the family?' Graham asked, with a sudden coolness descending over his manner. He was still smiling but the sentiment of the expression never touched his eyes.

'No,' Leighton replied, 'but she's my partner six days a week. We are as close as family.'

'And yet you don't know the patient – your partner's date of birth?'

'No, it seems like I don't.' Leighton's words sounded like a confession.

'Then I'm sorry, sir, admission to the intensive care ward is limited to close family only.' Graham was resolute in his rejection – if he had a shutter over the reception, Leighton felt sure he would have pulled it down.

'Is there anything else?' Graham asked curtly.

Leighton looked at his feet and took a breath. 'Look, my friend Alice she doesn't have any family,' he said quietly, 'if I don't show up to visit her, nobody will.'

'I'm sorry sir.' Graham said with another cool flash of his white smile. 'rules are rules – I really wish there was something I could do, but that are there to protect everyone.'

'Jesus, are you serious?' Leighton felt a flush of real anger.

'Yes I am, sir. Is there anything else I can help you with?'

'No,' Leighton said. He then turned around and began walking away. He had only taken four or five steps away from the reception desk when his pace slowed, and then he stopped. A phrase Alice had used echoed in his mind – *if you're doing the right thing, don't let assholes and difficulties get in your way.* After transferring the toy and the flowers to the same hand, Leighton reached into his shirt pocket. He then turned around and walked back to the desk.

Graham looked up again and was about to speak, when Leighton held up the badge to silence him.

'My name is officer Leighton Jones of Oceanside P. D. Badge 3386 I'm here on police business to see the victim of a major hit and run incident. The incident happened on Oceanside Boulevard, which is an area within my legal jurisdiction.

'But- '

'Right now, Graham, I would like to be directed to the victim's current location in this building. And if you fucking dare to wilfully deny or delay my legally enshrined access to the victim, I swear to almighty God I will charge you with obstruction of justice – which carries a penalty of a thousand dollar fine or at least a year in jail. So in a matter of seconds, I will cuff you, read your Miranda rights and drag your officious little ass to the station myself. So, what's it going to be?'

Graham nodded and began shuffling papers behind the reception. After a moment, he located the correct one and peered at it. 'She's on the third floor- Intensive Care – Room 2.10.'

'Thanks,' Leighton said and the began walking towards the elevators.

When the steel doors slid open on the second floor, Leighton stepped cautiously into a square shaped hallway with a glass door on each of the remaining three sides. He walked towards the one marked Intensive Care and it automatically swung silently inwards to reveal a small u-shaped seating area.

As he approached the orange plastic seats where a couple of worried looking visitors sat in nervous contemplation, Leighton was reminded of the police station waiting area back at Mission Avenue. They were both places where members of the public were suddenly confronted by the harsh realities of life. The difference was that he found a sense of security in the police station.

Before Leighton had a chance to take a seat, a tall nurse dressed entirely in white approached him.

'Can I help you?' she asked. Her expression revealed little emotion.

'I hope so, I'm here to see Annie Mead, if that's possible. I'm her partner at Oceanside P.D. I know it's outside of hours, but I'm the closest thing to family she has.'

The nurse looked at Leighton and for a moment seemed about to refuse him entry, but something in his haunted expression must have been enough to convince her that he was genuine.

'Okay, come with me.' she said, 'But no longer than a few minutes, okay.'

'Sure,' Leighton nodded gratefully, 'whatever you say.'

The nurse led Leighton along a corridor which had several open doors on both sides. As he passed each of these doorways Leighton glanced in to find patients who were sitting up watching small television sets, or lying back in a fog of medication.

Leighton smiled softly, thinking how if he was lucky, he might find Alice actually awake- or better still watching some of the daily shows and cursing at the television set.

Finally, they stopped at the end of the corridor where the door marked 2.10. Leighton felt a trickle of sweat slip down the inside of his collar.

'Here we are,' the nurse said. 'You can go in now. I'll be along at the station desk if you need anything.'

'Thanks,' Leighton said, but he was no longer paying attention to anything other than the prospect of seeing his friend. He knocked the wooden door gently and carefully pushed it open.

In the initial moments after stepping into the shaded room, Leighton was convinced that the nurse had led him to the wrong place. The shrunken, pale figure on the bed bore little resemblance to Alice. The amount of plastic tubes connected to her broken body made the person on the bed appear like some science fair experiment rather than a hospital patient. Her partially bandaged head looked as if it had been shaved, and the edges of crude black stitches could be seen like insect legs peeking out from beneath the fabric above one ear. The orange stain of the surgical iodine had left an unnatural orange mark on her cheek, which merged like a sunset into the purple bruising beneath Alice's left eye. Her nose and mouth were covered with a clear plastic mask to which a blue corrugated tube was attached. Perhaps, when she came round, Leighton could tell Alice that she had looked like an Air Force fighter pilot. He knew she would like that.

Nearing the bed, Leighton was unspeakably relieved to see the steady rise and fall of Alice's chest beneath the stark white bed sheet.

'Hey boss,' Leighton said softly.

There was not reply from the bed other than the regular. beep and sigh of the indifferent machines.

'I know you got a bit of a knock, but I need you back, okay' Leighton continued, 'you can't spend your last week of work lazing around here. Otherwise I'll just show up and annoy you every day. You hear me in there?'

If she did hear Leighton's words, Alice did not show it. The slowly rising of her chest and the regular pip of the heart monitor were the only indications that she was alive at all. Leighton shuffled his feet nervously. He wanted to reach out and touch her, but was afraid that even that small gesture would trigger a dramatic event or an alarm to sound. Instead, he placed the toy and flowers on the stiff bedsheets at her feet, and then babbled on for almost twenty minutes – during which time there was simply no response.

After Leighton left the hospital room, he stepped uncertainly into the corridor and found the nearest fire exit door. He pushed it open, feeling the resistance of the automatic closer, and then entered a large empty stairwell that smelled of disinfectant. Moving unsteadily to one side, he gripped the smooth black handrail and lowered himself on to the first step he could find. For a moment, he took a couple of deep breaths and tried to hold back the pain. It was futile.  Leighton buried his face in his hands and felt hot tears slid down the palms of his hands and scorched his wrists. His shoulders hitched up and down as he wept for his only friend.

## 34

An anger burned inside of Steve Brookes. Leona had not attended his afternoon class. As he began his lecture, he had glanced up to the place where Leona would usually sit, only to discover that she was missing. On a couple of occasions during the lecture, other students had arrived late and had tried to sneak discretely into the class. Steve had glanced anxiously at the door, hoping that one of the latecomers might be Leona, but he was left disappointed.

At the end of the lecture, he had stepped away from the podium to ask a couple of the other students if they had seen Leona. Steve deliberately tried to sound casual as his was an innocent enquiry, but his efforts were wasted- nobody seemed to know where she was.

This was not something Brookes had planned for. His well-rehearsed plan had involved engaging Leona in a conversation about her critical essay on Jefferson's opponents. He could then suggest that she had some really good ideas that he'd love to hear more about – perhaps over coffee or lunch. Flattery, he had discovered through practice, would often seal the deal.

But now Brookes' plans were unravelling before him, and he felt out of control- it was not a sensation he enjoyed.

He leaned on wooden the podium as the last of the students finally slowly drifted towards the exit of the lecture hall. Some young man hung back to ask the distracted lecturer if he was okay, but Brookes had simply nodded and waved them away with one hand.

It was in those moments, in the quiet lecture theatre, that Brookes realised he would need to take matters into his own hands. Clearly fate was testing him. He could either admit defeat and allow Leona to slip through his fingers, or he could tighten his grip. Brooke's decided on the latter.

After crossing the neat lawn between his office and the administration block, Brookes entered the student records building. And found himself facing a long glass fronted counter behind which three women and a man were busily taking calls and filing papers.

A petite woman with dark hair glanced up at Brookes than approached the part of the counter at which he stood. 'Can I help you?' she asked.

'I hope so,' Brookes said with a smile. 'My name is Stephen Brookes, I lecture in Humanities over in the Literature building and one of my students hasn't been able to attend class this week.'

'Oh, that's not good,' the receptionist said.

'I know,' Brookes said in a sympathetic tone, 'and to make matter worse, her friends have told me that she is really worried about falling behind so I'd like to drop some materials off to her. If that's okay? I don't need her to do anything, but I'd like her to have a copy of all the course materials.'

'Of course. That's so sweet of you. So I take it you are just looking for a term-time address?'

'Yes,' Brookes said. 'But, hey, only if it's okay. I don't want anyone getting into bother.'

'No, it's fine. You are staff after all. What is the student's name?'

'Leona Carlson.'

'Okay,' the woman said with a smile, 'if you give me a moment, I'll get her home address for you.'

Brookes couldn't help but grin. 'That would be perfect,' he said softly.

## 35

During the drive home through the bustling lanes of the hot city, Leighton made a silent commitment to do two specific things. The first was to actually talk to Heather and sort things out. Recent events meant that life seemed suddenly more tenuous and precious than it had the previous day. It seemed crazy to let relationships fall apart. The hard part was figuring out what to do. So, he thought about the ways in which he might make things easier between him and his wife. The upset of the day meant he really didn't have much appetite, but he was willing to make an effort. He thought that maybe they could go down to the pier for dinner – Heather could choose. They could order something nice, and perhaps he could just listen to Heather – really listen, the way he did when they had first got together. Maybe that would help to get things back on track – or at least get them closer to the right track. That seemed possible, and so Leighton parked that idea as a potential solution to his stalled marriage.

The second thing Leighton made a commitment to do was to keep moving forward with the Kelly Coombs investigation. His initial response was to simply throw the towel in and let the case fall apart. The truth would come out eventually, or perhaps never.

But the only thing Leighton could do for Alice until she got better was to carry on with her work. Alice would want that. In fact, if he didn't push on with the case, he knew for certain that as soon as she was up and able to speak, she would give him hell for wasting valuable time and failing to follow up on their leads. Alice was a person of action – so if Leighton was charting her path, he would need to assume her mantle.

Climbing the stairs to the apartment, Leighton could smell the aroma of onions frying from somewhere in the building. That was good, he thought. If Heather noticed his red eyes, Leighton could blame it on the vapour in the hallway. However, there was no need to prepare an explanation. When he opened the door to the apartment, Leighton found that the place was eerily quiet.

'Heather,' he called as he stepped inside 'you there, honey?'

Leighton padded through the short hallway to the living room. It was there that he found

a single sheet of paper lying on the coffee table. It had been folded in half but the air conditioning was still running, causing it to flutter half open into two arches like a pair of sea-gull's wings. Leighton walked over to the table and picked up the fluttering note. The material was a page torn from one of Heather's ruled notepads. As he picked up the note, Leighton had half expected it to be a list of items they needed from the grocery store, but it wasn't. The writing was neat and small:

*Leighton, I think a bit of time apart from each other would do us both some good right now. I am going to my parents' place for a couple days. Please don't call me. We can talk later.*

Each word felt like a punch to the guts.

Still holding the paper in his hand, Leighton walked through to the bedroom. It felt to him as if letting go of the note would somehow represent letting go of Heather, and yet he knew at some instinctive level their separation – however slow – was already in progress. It seemed to Leighton as if he was attempting to hold on to slippery hand of an exhausted swimmer. He loved Heather, but he felt that whatever unspoken barrier had grown between them was formidable. But Leighton didn't have the option of dwelling on the broken relationship. It was already pulling him down.

Sitting on the edge of the bed, he read the note again – carefully this time- as if the act of slowly scanning each word would somehow change the sentiment behind them. It made no difference.

Leighton knew that there was a dark crevice opening up in his life and if crawled too close to its edge, he would be drawn into it and would vanish into the darkness. With no close friends or family, the only option Leighton had was to bury himself in his job. Distraction, he figured, would be better than destruction.

Padding through to the living room, Leighton sat down on the couch with a bottle of beer and a legal pad. After picking up a pen, he began to scratch out notes:

*Amy-lee Hollander 17, found dead in pool*

*Kelly aged 21, female, found dead – car dumped in water.*

*Sarah 21, female, found dead – car dumped in water.*

*Witness sees a red car at point at Windmill Lake at the point at which second victim's car went into water.*

*Witness two sees a red car at the point at which Kelly's car went into the water.*

*Amy-Lee lived across the street from Brookes.*

*Kelly Attended class with Brookes. Witness heard him confess to an interest in her.*

*Sarah worked in coffee shop frequented by Brookes and was offered tuition by him.*

Picking up the bottle, Leighton put it to his mouth and then took a deep drink. The fizzing bubbles filled his mouth and he swallowed. He then narrowed his eyes and scanned his notes.

There was something elusive about all of the details. Like a jigsaw puzzle with half the pieces missing.

Leighton then remembered another detail and wrote it down.

*Both cars had driver's mirror turned all the way around.*

It was easy to view all of these facts as significant and interconnected, but Leighton was also now aware of the counter argument that each of these were insignificant or simply coincidental. Leighton was pulled from his thoughts by the shrill ringing of the telephone. He groaned as he got up from the sofa and walked stiffly through to the kitchen.

'Hello?' he said into the handset. He had fully expected to hear Heather's voice, but he was wrong.

'Officer Leighton Jones?' The voice sounded dry and croaky.

'Yep,'

'My name is Detective Ray Brander at Westmorland Police Department on Salton Sea. I picked up a message saying you had called up asking about female homicide victims in the area?'

'That's right,' Leighton said.

'Okay, firstly can I ask why you left a private number rather than the Oceanside station one?'

'Sure,' Leighton said, trying to sound casual, 'I just wanted to keep it on the down low. At least until I was sure there was anything to pursue.'

'Hmm,' Brander sounded a little unconvinced. 'You got a badge number there, officer Jones?'

'It's three-seven-six-five.'

'You Homicide or Vice?'

Leighton tried to infer from the tone of voice which of the two was preferable. It was impossible.

'Neither, I work Traffic?' Leighton said quickly.

'Traffic?' Brander let out dry chuckle. 'So what the fuck are you doing sniffing around murder victims for anyways?'

'Well, we found a couple of dead girls in two separate cars down here in Oceanside. One potential suspect used to live over on Salton Lake. I just figured if there had been similar cases there, it might add some weight when putting a case together.'

'Look kid, can I offer you a word of advice.'

'Sure.'

'Don't step on the toes off Homicide detectives. We don't take kindly to amateurs trampling over our cases. You'll never get anywhere in this line of work doing that.'

'I hear you. I was more thinking that I didn't want to bother anyone with my theory unless it was worth bothering them about.'

'Well, kid, it looks like today's your lucky day.'

'How's that?'

'The only reason your message only ended on my desk because I'm a few weeks away from retirement and the assholes in charge up here think that I have nothing left to offer except clearing out filing cabinets and answering calls. Their loss is your gain. I left the trash-bags to the janitors and then did a little digging for you.'

'You did?' Leighton couldn't believe that he might be making some progress.

'Sure, but don't get your pecker up just yet. The time-frame you gave us was early eighty-two to late eighty-five, that right?'

'Yeah,' Leighton replied.

'Well, I'm pleased to tell you that there were no homicides of any sort male or female in the area during that window. In fact, the only murder we had was during a fucked up gas station robbery on Bannister Road in eighty-two and that was only because the young punk panicked and fired two rounds into the cashier who was emptying the cash register just as he was told to.'

'Jeez! Well, thanks for checking it out.'

'Whoa, hold your horses a second, son.'

'There's more?'

'Yeah. Look, it may be nothing. We have an open missing persons case from eighty-two, young woman named Ellie Johnstone. At the time of her disappearance Ellie was renting a trailer close to Redhill Marina. I've always figured somebody from outside of town was involved.'

'Did she live alone?'

'No, she was cohabiting with Dwayne Barclay- a two-bit local dirtbag. To tell you truth a lot of people thought he was involved in her dropping off the grid, but I didn't buy that.'

'Why?'

'He was the one reported her missing the morning after she failed to come home? I know Barclay wasn't the smartest guy in town, but if he had done something to his wife, it would seem a little crazy to invited the cops out to crawl all over his home the next day.'

'What was the situation?'

'Ellie worked as a waitress in the Red Lantern inn three miles North from their trailer park. On the night she vanished, she finished her shift at 10.30 and left for home in an old grey Dodge that was registered in her name. Some other staff and customers all saw her leave, but she never arrived home – or anywhere else.'

'So, the woman and her car are missing?'

'Yeah, that about sums it up. I'm not dumb enough to hurry to chalk this one up as a homicide, but still it feels a little bit weird to me. Westmorland isn't a big station – most of the people who work here live in the area. I would have expected that in all the years since eighty-six, we would have heard something about Ellie Johnstone, or her car would have been found nose down in some ravine – but there's been nada.'

'Seems a little strange,' Leighton said.

'Yeah, but by the time you get to my stage, you realise that there's a whole lot of strange out there in the world – doesn't always mean that there was a crime at the end of every lead.'

'Thanks for filling me in anyway,' Leighton said.

'It's fine, kid. I can have the details faxed over to you at Oceanside in the morning. They have a machine for doing that here in the office but that's one piece of technology I'm happy to leave to the young guns. Should be with you by lunchtime.'

'I'd appreciate that Detective Brander.'

'Yeah, well just remember I ain't saying the girl was murdered, just that it's maybe worth considering that if we had a dirt-bag up here for a while, they may have been involved.'

'Sure, I'll add to the list of potential leads.'

'You make sure you do. And then do yourself a favour and hand everything you've got over to the experts.'

'I will,' Leighton said.

'Glad to hear it.'

'And good luck with the retirement.'

'Thanks, kid. After two decades working the streets, I'll need all the luck I can get just to stay sober and stay alive.'

There was a sharp click as Brander hung up leaving Leighton standing in the empty kitchen, phone in hand, and wondering about how it must feel to be at the end of a police career. He wondered if he would ever be happy to retire, when the time finally arrived.

After he replaced his own phone on the wall mount, Leighton walked back to the living room and slowly sat down on the small sofa. He rubbed his hands across his face, and then picked up his notepad. When he looked the facts in black and white, it seemed pretty likely that the cases of the two local females were connected. However, when he added the missing woman from Salton See into the mix, it seemed pretty scary. They all involved young women who vanished in their cars.

But without Alice there to guide him, Leighton felt suddenly out of his depth and sinking.

The evidence seemed to be starting to add up, but it also seemed that there was no point taking it to Daniels if had already made up his mind that both girls had taken their own lives.

He therefore decided that he would take it to the chief and see what he advised. Alice had worked under five different chiefs and she regularly told Leighton that the current one was the best.

Apparently, he had been a fairly decent cop who had worked his way up

## 36

From where Steve was squatting just off a dusty road on the hillside he had the perfect view.

As he sat on the warm ground, with his binoculars in his hands, he could peer directly into the private gardens of the properties of the Orchard Road. The one he was focussed on was a large corner property. It was two storey house, built from red brick, with an adjoining garage and a long teardrop shaped swimming pool. There was no escape from the hot sun out here on the baked landscape. Brookes felt a trickle of sweat run down his neck as he watched Leona sunbathing on a white plastic lounger, which was draped in a yellow towel. Her swimsuit was bright orange and, in Brookes opinion, served to enhance her caramel coloured skin. He licked his lips as he watched the girl, his eyes crawling over every inch of her skin.

Then, whilst in the midst of his fantasy, some self-preservation mechanism must have kicked in, because Brookes had the sudden urge to lower his binoculars. It was then that his peripheral vision picked up motion, and he instinctively turned his head. From area to Brookes' left, a lone figure was approaching. The rippling heat haze made the figure initially unclear, but after a moment, Brooker realised it was a police officer. He was dressed in uniform and wearing mirrored sunglasses, as he kicked up little puffs of dust whilst crossing the arid ground.

Eventually, when he drew close to Brookes, the officer called out.

'Good afternoon, sir.'

'Hey,' officer.' Brookes said as he stood up, bag in hand. 'What can I do for you?'

'I found a car left by the roadside just down the road there. Would that be your vehicle?'

'Yes sir, it is.'

'Can I ask what you're doing out here?'

'Sure, officer.' Brookes smiled, 'I come out here for the wildlife.'

'The wildlife?' The cop didn't sound too convinced, but then Brookes added the best part.

'Can I show you what's in my bag?'

'Sure, just open though, don't reach in.'

'Of course.' Brookes nodded, opened the bag and held it out for the officer to see. Inside were a couple of guides to wild plants and insects. Brookes had purchased them specially for just such an encounter.

'I lecture over at the college in San Diego every day,' Brookes continued, 'so when my shift is over I have pretty much had enough of people and come out here. You must know what it's like in your job, officer.'

'Yeah, I just prefer an empty pool hall to the side of a dusty road.'

'I guess I'm just a little weird,' Brookes said with a self-effacing shrug.

'Well, regardless what you're doing, you need to move your car. It's a potential hazard.'

'Of course, officer. I only stopped there because I thought I saw a Condor flying around the rocks over here.'

'As I said, I just need that car moved.'

The cop then stood still and watched as Brookes picked his way over the rocks back towards his car. He could easily have walked with him, but the cop didn't want to spend any more time in the guy's company than necessary. There was just something about the guy didn't quite add up. It was almost like watching some insect making its way across the dusty ground. Perhaps that's why the guy was so interested in collecting insects, because he himself resembled a spider.

## 37

Leighton was a sitting opposite the Chief, waiting in silence whilst the man peered at a sheet of paper upon which was a list of evidence pointing to Brookes' guilt.

'And this is your theory – that a college teacher is running around Oceanside killing young women and dumping their cars in bodies of water?'

'Yes, it is.'

'And you are aware that Homicide are considering the two deaths to be unrelated suicides?'

'I am, sir.'

'So what makes you so sure that they weren't?'

'Steven Brookes knew both these young women.'

'So what? He's a college professor,' the chief said and waved his hand as if swatting an invisible fly. 'His job would suggest that he knows hundreds of women every single day.'

'Yeah, but a car matching his was also seen in both locations prior to the deaths.'

'Oceanside is a big place; there will be hundreds of cars that match his.'

'But, that's not all, sir. A girl a few houses along from his home was found dead in her pool last year – she looked just like the other two young women.'

'Is that it?'

'No, there's more. A couple of years ago, Brookes spent some time living up in a trailer park on the edge of Salton Sea. Just before he moved down to Oceanside, his neighbour went missing.'

'Well, as I said, that could also be-'

'She was described as being a blonde and in her early twenties, just exactly like the two girls we have lying on the slab over on Minnesota Avenue and the one buried in Eternal Hills.'

The chief looked a little like someone who had just been sucker-punched.

'Look, even if this guy Brookes knew both girls and someone else who went missing, it doesn't mean much. How's his record – any previous charges or warrants?'

'No, it's clean. But I have a witness from the college who is prepared to state for the record that Brookes was pursuing a relationship with Kelly Coombs.'

The captain sighed. 'This sounds like a whole lot of conjecture to me.'

'Sir, when I was first put with her you told me that Officer Mead was one of the best cops you'd ever known – that she had a cop's instinct and I could learn much from her.'

'That's very true.'

Leighton nodded. 'Well, she believed that Brookes was involved in this case. I know that if she wasn't laid up in the tri-county hospital right now, she would be pursuing this guy. You know she would!'

The chief sighed, and then pinched the bridge of his nose. 'Okay, I'll tell you what, I'll talk to Daniels – ask him to bring this college guy in, and see what he has to say for himself. But I'll agree only as a favour to Alice, and when this guy walks back out of the interview room, I want you to drop the matter. How does that sound?'

'Thanks, sir. I'd really appreciate that.' Leighton said.

'Okay. What have you got on the schedule today?'

'Two Driver Awareness classes. One this morning and the other in the afternoon.'

'You able to do that on your own, or do you want me to draft somebody else in? Sanchez could do it- he's stood in before?''

'It's okay sir, I'm happy to take it on my own.

'You sure?'

'Yeah,' Leighton nodded. He would prefer it that way.

## 38

Leighton was carefully placing sheets of paper printed with road diagrams on the eight desks of the Traffic Teaching room when the door slammed open. He looked to see Jim Daniels storm in. Daniels' face was red with anger and vein on his left temple looked engorged. He walked up to Leighton with his chest puffed out. Leighton would have found it comical if it didn't look so much like the other man was about to lose his shit.

'So, what the fuck did you think you were doing, talking to the chief about my investigation, huh?'

'I just had a theory.' Leighton said softly. 'It was only a conversation.'

'Oh a theory. Okay Einstein. So why the hell didn't you bring it to me?'

'You're right, I probably should've.'

'No shit!'

'I just thought-'

'Whoa! The issue is that you didn't fucking think at all. Now, I have to go to go pick this guy up – as a witness – not a suspect, and then I am going to ask him a few questions. And do you know what'll happen after that?'

Leighton shook his head.

'I'll let him go. And if he decides to sue for harassment it can be your name on the document, not mine.'

Leighton thought about saying something but decided to let Daniels fire burn itself out. It seemed like the right call.

Having said his piece, Daniels stormed out, leaving the papers to drift like oversized confetti to the floor.

## 39

Steve Brookes was sitting in his car trying to figure out a new way to get close to Leona. Eventually, he decided that he would start jogging in her street. That way he could be in the area without arousing any suspicion. Plus, Leona was clearly into sport, so Steve would simply up his game – literally. Feeling a buzz of excitement, Brookes was starting to open his car door when a whoop of a siren blared out.

He twisted his head to see a brown saloon car pulled up behind him with a flashing red light on the vehicle's dashboard.

Steve hesitated for a moment then climbed out of his car., by which time a detective in a grey suit was already walking towards him.

A friendly smile instinctively slid across Steve's face.

'Can I help you?' he asked.

'Stephen James Brookes?' Daniels asked.

'Yes. What's this all about?'

'We'd like to speak to you about a case we are investigating.'

'Certainly, can we go inside? I can fix us both a drink.' He made as if to step towards the house, but Daniels reached out and grabbed his arm.

'We'd prefer to have the discussion down at the station.' Daniels said. His tone of voice made it sound almost like an invitation, but the vice like grip in which held Brookes arm suggest it was not optional.

'I see.' Brookes nodded. 'Do I perhaps have time for a quick shower?'

'We would like to go now,' Daniels said firmly, then added 'If you don't mind.'

'And if I say no?'

'Well, then would seek approval to arrest you, then come back and do just that.'

'But if I come with you just now, I am not under arrest?'

'Exactly.' Daniels said slowly as if speaking to child.

It was as Brookes took a step towards the waiting police car that the screen door clattered open and Lina rushed out of the house.

'What the hell's going on?' she shouted.

On the opposite side of the street, a passing paperboy wearing a Goonies T-shirt had stopped to watch the drama unfold.

'It's nothing,' Steve said as an officer opened the back door of the police car for him. 'One of the students from my faculty was found dead. I'm going down to the station to tell them what I know.'

'But what's that got to do with you?' Lina asked her voice nearing on panic.

'Don't worry. They probably want to talk to all of the faculty – my name will just be first alphabetically.'

Daniels was getting ready for a total shit show, but for that moment at least Mrs Brookes seemed to buy her husband's fictitious explanation.

'Okay,' she said reluctantly, 'can I tag along too?'

'I'm afraid that's not possible,' Daniels said. 'We need to interview witnesses on their own. But he's a big boy – I'm sure he will be okay.'

'So, how long will he be gone?'

'We will get your husband back to you as soon as we can Mr Brookes,' At that point he sounded like he believed that, but having already wasted more time than he wanted to, Daniels quickly led Brookes to the car and deposited him inside.

After she had watched the police car glide away from her home, Lina walked back into her home and closed the door. She leaned back against the solid wood for a moment. She then walked into the relative privacy of her bedroom where she stood in the centre of the room and screamed. The sound was harsh, guttural and painful. It was the sound of loss and fear.

Steve Brookes had been the only man she had ever loved. Even the first time she saw him, skipping hurrying into the lecture room during her first semester at William Jessop University she knew they would end up together, not married perhaps, but certainly together. He had an aura, a musky charisma that was almost intoxicating. Whilst the other men she had encountered were bland and perfunctory, Steve was glittering with charm and wit. She would do anything for him, but it seemed that at the moment in the silent house there was nothing she could do for him. It was this blunt certainty which shook Lina Brookes from her stupor. Steve was at the mercy of whatever lies the corrupt cops chose to believe but she knew something felt wrong. Steve was keeping secrets, and whilst Lina was reluctant to discuss these with him, the cops might not be so hesitant.

For a while, she paced the room, twisting her hands together as she tried to unravel the web of madness which seemed to be forming around her.

Eventually, she concluded that she should get herself cleaned up and presentable, then drive down to the station to wait for him. It would be better that her came home in her car than some stinking cop car.

It was only after her shower, when was wrapped in a white towel that Lina stepped into the walk–in wardrobe that she discovered her husband's secret.

Lina had been about to open a drawer and pull out her underwear when she absently glanced at her reflection in a tall freestanding mirror. Her skin was golden – a natural consequence of the Californian sun- but her eyes looked wrinkled and tired- as if she was coming down with some sickness.   Perhaps she was. God only knew that her husband's coolness towards her had taken its toll on her physically and psychologically.  It was then, in that moment, that Lina partially turned away from the mirror and noticed the triangular corner of the box. It was peeking out from the space beneath the shelves like the beak of some strange squat bird. Lina frowned in confusion, and then moved as if in a trance away from the mirror and towards her unsettling discovery.

Kneeling down on the caramel coloured carpet, Lina reached beneath the bottom shelf and pulled out the box that her husband had failed to fully conceal. It sat on the floor in front of Lina's naked knees, like an unwanted gift.

After carrying it through to the bedroom, Lina placed the box upon the bed and then stood up. She returned to the wardrobe and quickly got dressed. Her adrenaline levels were already beginning to spike as she left the bedroom and immersed herself with the normal business of maintaining her home. But eventually, after every floor had been mopped, every surface, bleached and unnecessarily polished, Lina could no longer distract herself. She walked slowly back into the bedroom, and stood looking down at the box on her bed as if it was an intruder. Even as the sun began to fade, filling the room with a dull red glow, Lina Brookes did not move from the place. She was held in some dark fascination by the object on the bed. She simultaneously did and did not want to know what her husband kept hidden in the box. So finally, as the sky faded to black, Steve Brookes' wife looked inside her husband's box of mementos...

40

Detective Daniels and Detective Charlie Ross sat across from Steven Brookes in interview room number 3 of Oceanside Police Station. The room was small and contained nothing more than a table-bolted to the floor- and three chairs. Daniels was pissed off at having being told to interview someone by the captain, but he had to admit there was something unsettling about the guy who was sitting opposite him.

Steve was wearing a peach coloured t-shirt, white shorts and had a pair of black Wayfairer sunglasses perched on his head. Daniels thought that the smug prick looked more like he was visiting a country club rather than being questioned about a murder enquiry. The smell of Armani cologne coming off him was also almost suffocating in the small space.

'Okay Mr Brookes, thank you for agreeing to be interviewed.' Daniels smiled, but his expression didn't reach his eyes. He was keen to get this whole thing out of the way.

'Why wouldn't I?' Brookes said with a shrug of his shoulders, 'I already told you I have nothing to hide, Jim. Can I call you Jim?'

'No. Detective Daniels or simply Detective will do.'

'Okay, Detective.' Brookes said solemnly.

'So, as you know, we are investigating the deaths of two young women – Kelly-Anne Coombs and Sarah Levin. At this stage, the investigation is ongoing so the purpose of this interview is only to help piece things together. So, can I ask in what capacity did you know Kelly Coombs?'

'Well, I believe she was a student at the college where I work.'

Daniels nodded and ticked a list of points on a sheet of paper in front of him.

'What are you ticking?' Brookes asked.

'Just confirming the facts,' Daniels said. 'Was Kelly in any of your specific classes?'

Brookes narrowed his eyes and glanced upwards as if struggling to recall. 'You know; I believe she may have been. I'd really have to check. Jim, I'm sure you can appreciate what it's like working with the public. I literally see hundreds of students every single day. And the older you get, the more these kids all start to all look the same.'

Daniels nodded. 'Mr Brookes I'd appreciate it if you don't call me Jim.'

'Oh, sure. Sorry, Detective.' Brooked held up his hands. 'Hell, I'm just being friendly – sorry.'

'So, according to college records, Kelly – who you can't quite remember- has been in your American Colonial History class for two years.'

Something dark flickered briefly across Brookes' face and was gone. 'Yeah, well like I said I teach many students, so It's possible, I suppose,' he said.

'How many students would you say are in that class?'

'Well, it's difficult to say.' Brookes frowned as if deep in thought. 'I really couldn't say.'

'Try.' Daniels persisted. He noted with a sense of accomplishment that a couple of dark patches were starting to for in the armpits of Brooker's shirt.

'Jeez, sixty, maybe a little bit less.'

'The faculty secretary – Mrs Marion Klein- told me that there are two classes, each made up of twenty-two students. Does that sound about right?'

'Yeah, I suppose.' Brookes looked at his nails.

'So, Kelly would be one of forty-four students you teach.'

'I've agreed with you already.' Brookes said sharply, 'She's in the class – sure.'

'Okay, what about Sarah Levin?'

'Who?'

Daniels- who had interviewed hundreds of suspects throughout his time in homicide was an observant man. When he mentioned the name to Brookes, he noticed some small, almost imperceptible response in the man's eyes. It was just a small flicker as if he felt the sudden urge to look away but fought it. Daniels decided to use her name again.

'Sarah Levin, she is the second dead girl. We found her body in a car up on Whelan Lake.'

'Oh, right. Was she another student at USD? I'm sorry, I don't recall that name.'

'Sarah wasn't a student; she worked at The Gingerbread House coffee shop in the College Plaza Shopping Centre. I understand you stop by there quite regularly?'

'Yeah, I know the place,' Brookes conceded. 'But I only go there sometimes. Maybe once or twice in any month. I mean I wouldn't say I ever went there *regularly*.'

Daniels nodded, but did not note anything down. It was quickly becoming apparent that something wasn't quite adding up. He had fully expected the teacher to say that he knew both girls and was perhaps a little upset at their deaths. After that, he would let the guy go and thank him for co-operating in the investigation. He had even rehearsed what he would say to Jones when informing him of the colossal waste of time. But none of that was playing out the way the detective had expected.

Instead, the guy seemed to be trying to create some kind of smoke screen by denying he ever really knew the girls. Something about that just didn't feel right – it didn't mean the guy was a killer, but it was causing some alarm bells to ring for Daniels.

'I'd like to show you a photograph of Sarah Levin, would that be okay?'

Brookes suddenly appeared to be rattled, and he began to massage the back of his neck with one hand. 'The picture isn't of... you know of after she-?'

'No, Mr Brookes,' Daniels said deliberately. 'The picture I would like you to look at was taken from her drivers' licence – when she was alive.'

'Oh right, then sure,' Brookes nodded. 'It's just I've never seen a dead person before. I didn't want to be all freaked out.'

'No, we wouldn't want you freaking out.' Daniels took a small brown envelope from beneath his notepad, opened a flap on it and removed a copy of the woman's photograph. The image had been blown up to fill the entire page. He pushed the sheet of paper to Brookes. 'Does the woman in this picture look familiar to you?'

Brookes glanced at the sheet, for a second then shook his head.

'Sorry, no – that person doesn't seem familiar.'

It was officer Malcolm's turn to speak. 'A car matching your one was seen within the vicinity of where both bodies were recovered. Could you think of any reason to explain that?'

Brookes nodded for a moment as processing what he had heard. 'It's a popular car, what can I say?'

Daniels folded his arms. 'Let me just check that I understand this correctly, Mr Brookes. You say that you never had any real connection with Kelly and that you never knew Sarah.

'That's correct,' Brookes said with casual shrug.

'Okay,' Daniels nodded, can ask your shoe size?'

'Excuse me?'

'What size do you take in shoes?'

'Forty- six, why?'

'As I said, we're trying to rule you out of the investigation.'

'Or in?' Brookes said. This time he didn't smile.

'It's the same thing, Mr Brookes.'

'Not from where I'm sitting.'

Daniels was not going to get side-tracked, and carried on with his line of questioning. 'Mr Brookes are you familiar with the brand of running shoes Nike Air?'

'Yes, I guess.'

'And do you own a pair of these shoes?'

'What, you brought me over here to ask me about my tennis shoes? Come on detective, this is getting stupid now. I mean how long have we been doing this – it feels like we've been here for hours.'

'It's been twelve minutes. So, do you own a pair of them?' Daniels held his steel pen firmly gripped in one hand like a dagger.

'Sure, I believe I own a pair of them.' Brookes grinned, 'pretty much like every guy between the ages of thirteen and seventy-five. So, I doubt that means anything.'

'Yeah, those shoes certainly are quite popular.' Daniels conceded. 'Would you be willing to hand those shoes over to us?'

Brookes face seem to freeze for a second or two, and then he smiled and shook his head.

'You know what? I think I did own a pair but I believe I threw them out a while back.

Daniels knew that he might have just secured the first piece of physical evidence linking Brookes directly to the crime scene. Casts taken from the lagoon and the water treatment plant could be compared, and the shoes could be tested for soil and sand traces, but that would depend on having a strong enough affidavit to convince a judge to grant a warrant.

He, of course said nothing of this. Instead, he reached across and retrieved the photograph. He then efficiently gathered his notes into a single pile.

'So, is that it, we all done here?' Brookes asked. He let out a sigh.

Daniels said nothing.

'I'm free to go now, right?' Brookes asked.

'Not just yet, Mr Brookes. I want to run a couple of things by my boss, and then we can figure out If we need anything else from you.'

'What does that mean?'

'Detective Ross and I are just going to step out for a couple of minutes. Can we get you anything – a coffee, some water?'

Brookes shook his head.

'Okay, we hopefully won't be too long.

The two detectives stood up and then left the room.

## 41

Lina Brookes gripped the edge of the porcelain sink and threw up for the second time in five minutes. The faucet was running washing the mangled remains of her partially digested lunch away into the darkness of the plughole. Even as the retching subsided, Lina remained holding on to the glossy lip of the sink, trying to steady herself as if she were on some lurching ship.

In the bedroom behind her, the discarded box lay on the floor. All around it random items were scattered- a scarf, an earring, a lipstick, three pieces of underwear – none of which belonged to Lina.

Her husband had not only betrayed her with his sick desires, he had obviously enjoyed building his twisted little collection of mementos.

For the first time in her life, she felt terrified. If the police were looking for evidence of her husband's having something to do with missing girls, this Nike shoe-box was a fucking treasure chest. And at that point, in the grip of madness and confusion, Lina Brookes was tempted to drive down to the station and hand her weak husband's box of tricks over to the cops.

## 42

After he closed the door of the interview room. Daniels led the other officer along a narrow corridor lined with antidrug posters to a small room in which the chief was waiting. The room was almost empty except for a large Grundig television on a metal trolley. Captain Billings stood with his arms folded and a frown on his face as he stared at the video feed from the interview room.

'Well?' Daniels said as he nodded towards the image of Brookes on the screen.

'He's a cool bastard, I'll give you that. What do you reckon is going on?' Billings asked.

'He's lying about knowing the girls, that's for sure. But I can't tell whether he's simply covering up for his interest in them, or if it's something more. Witness statements about a car won't stand up in court – not without a definite license plate.'

'Has he mentioned a lawyer yet?'

'No, luckily. I reckon he's cocky enough to believe he can fool us without any help.'

'Good! So where does that leave us?' the Billings asked?

'We could go for a Polygraph? Add some weight to the plea for a warrant.'

Billings sighed. 'Come on Jim, you know it won't be admissible. It didn't do us any good last month with the Fleischer case.'

'Yeah, I know, but we don't need to treat it as evidence- just to point out where the inconsistencies in his version of events are and then, if the affidavit works, we can go dig into them.'

'You'd need to get him to agree to it.'

'I can get him to do that,' Daniels said with a wink.

Brookes was still staring at his hands when the door opened. He had been expecting that Daniels would appear and then simply tell him he was free to go, but that didn't happen. Instead, the detective didn't even enter the room; he just remained in the doorway and offered up a smile.

'Mr Brookes, I'm keen to see you back home, but a couple of things don't stack up as neatly as I'd like yet.'

'Well, what do you need to know?'

'Just a couple of points I want to go over. Would you be willing to take a polygraph test?'

'You mean a lie detector?' Something shifted in Brooke's expression. 'Why? I can answer any questions you have.'

'I'm sure you could but, it would just help rule you out of our enquiries for good. It proves what you have been saying is true.'

'What if I refuse?'

'Nobody can force you.' Daniels put his hands in his pockets to appear deliberately casual. 'But this could be an easy way to confirm what you have already told us.'

'What if the readings are wrong? I have heard that sometimes they make mistakes.

'Exactly, that's why they aren't used in court as evidence. So you don't need to worry – you can't incriminate yourself.'

'How long will it take?'

'We can have a guy here in twenty to thirty minutes-the recording will take less than an hour.'

'I really don't want be here too long; I have work for tomorrow's college classes that I need to prepare.'

'Look, how about if we cut it down to a couple of questions.'

'Okay, but I'd like something to eat first.'

'I'll get that organised for you,' Daniels said with a smile and closed the door.

Brookes was lost in some private recollection about Leona lying by her swimming pool. He was imagining sitting by her side, rubbing sunscreen into her warm smooth skin. It was as Brookes was fantasising about Leona's tanned flesh, that the door of the interview room opened and a female officer carrying a plastic tray entered. The officer who was petite with her blonde hair pulled back into a neat pony tail, smiled as she paused for a moment until the automatic door closer had done its job.

Brookes felt momentarily knocked off balance – it was as if his fantasy and reality were suddenly fusing together in some irresistible cocktail. He could almost feel his eyes physically widening as he stared at the female officer.

'Hi there, I've got some lunch for you,' she said as she approached the table.

As the officer grew near, Brookes could detect the faintest scent of a sweet perfume from her. An image of her dabbing it on her neck and wrists flashed through his mind, perhaps she would have been standing in her underwear as she did so.

'Thank you that's great,' Brookes smiled. 'What is it?'

'Just a couple of packs of sandwiches. Detective Daniels asked me to grab you some lunch.     I wasn't sure what you'd prefer – so there's roast chicken or cream cheese – oh, and some fruit.' She placed the plastic tray on the surface in front of Brookes.

'You're very kind. Officer-?' He peered at her golden name badge. 'Duncan.'

'Just doing my job,' the officer said with a brief smile. 'Is there anything else you need?'

Brookes looked down at his feet for a moment. 'Well, Officer Duncan was going to ask if – no it'll sound really dumb...'

'It's okay,' the officer said, 'I'm here to help. What do you need?'

'I was going to ask if someone could hang around here for a moment whilst I ate. Perhaps Officer Daniels?'

'Sure, I can ask, but I think he's upstairs sorting out a polygraph for you?'

'Perhaps you could then?' Brookes looked at her and raised his eyebrows hopefully. 'It honestly won't take long. It's just that I hate eating alone – always have. Luckily, we have a shared faculty lunch room over at the college, so there's always company at lunchtimes.'

'I'm not sure. We are not supposed to eat with witnesses.'

'Well, we don't need to talk about the missing women. In any case, I feel like I've already told your colleague everything I know.'

'I'll go check.'

'Please,' Brookes said with smile.

'Look, I could stay for a few minutes, but then I need to cover reception.'

'A few minutes would be prefect,' Brookes said with an easy and practised manner. 'Please, take a seat.'

Jodie Duncan was no fool. As she sat down opposite Stephen Brookes, she knew the guy was a sleaze-ball and possibly worse than that too, but she also knew that if was busy drooling over her while he ate his sandwiches, the guy might just be relaxed enough to slip up and disclose something useful, plus it would buy Daniels more time to secure the lie-detector.

Brookes opened the pack of sandwiches and held half of it out towards Jodie.

'Would you like to split these with me – there's much more than I can manage.'

'No thanks' Jodie said politely, 'We don't eat whilst on duty.'

'It'll be okay; I won't tell the boss,' Steve said in a mock whisper.

'No, it's fine, really.' Jodie laughed.

'Please yourself,' Steve said and then bit into it. He chewed over his food, still looking at Jodie, and then finally spoke again. 'You know; your whole face lights up when you laugh. I would never have guessed.'

'Guessed what?' Jodie asked.

'That you were a cop.'

'Cops can smile too you know.'

'So what made you join the police department?'

'My dad was a cop,' Jodie said proudly.

'Was?' Brookes raised his eyebrows.

'Yeah, he retired last year. He and my mom moved to Florida. I looked at his life and thought it didn't look too shabby. I mean he gets to spend his sixties on little boat, fishing for Black-fin Tuna.'

'Sounds pretty good,' Steve nodded and then took a sip of water. 'I know how calming getting out on the water can be. I used to have a little boat myself.'

'Down at the harbour?'

'No, this was a while back when I lived out at Salton Sea.'

At that point, the door opened and Daniels entered.

'Okay Mr Brookes, we have everything set up for you.'

## 43

Leighton entered the small refreshment area of the police station and approached the coffee maker. This area which mainly used by officer on working back-to-back shifts, was a long room featuring eight square tables, a random selection of orange plastic chairs and three humming vending machines. The coffee however was free and provided in the form of two temperamental sunbeam filter machines. Most officers knew to always use the machine on the left as- unlike the other one- it at least heated up the coffee to a little more than blood temperature.

An older detective- named Joe Stillie- from homicide was sitting at one of the tables. In front of him was a half-eaten burrito and a can of 7-up.

'Hey,' he called across to Leighton, 'any more news on how Alice is doing?'

'I just got off the phone to the hospital.' Leighton said as he tipped the contents of the coffee pot into a paper cup. 'They said she's still out of it. I guess these things just take time.'

'She's a tough old bird,' the detective said almost to himself, 'If there's a way to pull through, Alice Mead will find it.'

Both men were silent for a moment, then the detective glanced up at Leighton who had taken a small sip from his cup.

'So, I heard on the grapevine that you somehow managed to piss Jim Daniels off this morning.'

'Yeah,' Leighton said, 'he made his feelings clear, but he was justified.'

'How come?'

'I got hot-headed and took some information straight to the chief instead of running it by him. Jumped the chain of command. Won't happen again.'

Joe took a sip from his can and then nodded. 'Well, don't beat yourself up too much, sometimes we all need a kick in the pants to get us moving. Anyways, it sounds like the suspect you picked out might be involved after all.'

'How do you know?' Leighton asked.

'I heard that Daniels and Malcolm Ross have been questioning him, but sounds like he's a smartass. Insists he's innocent. Very confident and relaxed. The prick even agreed to take a lie detector test. Pete Billings is in strapping him up as we speak.'

'Yeah?' Leighton was surprised things had progressed so quickly.

'That's what they're saying. And I can tell you for a fact that Daniels would never push for a lie detector if he didn't already have something solid to go on. If you go up there, you might get a bit more info.'

Leighton threw his cup in the trash and then rubbed his hands together. 'Thanks, but I have a class of DUIs to take, plus I don't want push Daniels closer to the edge. Once a day is enough'

'Very wise,' the older cop said with a chuckle. 'Alice has trained you well.'

## 44

Leighton had only just finished leading a driver awareness class in the station teaching room when he received an unexpected visitor. He had stacked most of the eight plastic chairs into a corner of the room, and was in the process of wiping down the board when Jim Daniels appeared in the doorway. He knocked on the wooden doorframe to get Leighton's attention.

'You got a minute?' he said with a calmer tone than earlier that day.

'Sure,' Leighton said as he continued wiping road diagrams off the board. He braced himself for another outburst from Daniels, but that wasn't what followed. Instead, Daniels offered Leighton a small self-conscious smile.

'Look, buddy I just wanted to say sorry, about earlier. The chief caught me off guard, asking me to bring in somebody who didn't even feature in the investigation.' Daniels said. 'I guess I felt I'd been side-lined- left out of the loop.'

'Don't worry about it,' Leighton replied, 'You were right. I should've come to you with everything I had. It won't happen again.'

Daniels nodded, and then rubbed the back of his neck. 'Well, that's good to know. Anyway, with Alice out of commission for a few weeks, I just thought I'd give you the good news.

'What's that?' Leighton asked.

'We interviewed Brookes, and it seems that he caught himself out.'

'He did?' Leighton asked. It seemed surprising given his experience of interviews.

'Yeah, we hooked him up to a lie detector. He's a cool cucumber and was doing fine until Billings asked him where he was at the time we estimated that each of the girls died.'

'What did he say?' Leighton asked.

'Brookes gave us the same answer for both nights- claimed that he was at home watching baseball on TV with his wife.'

'Did it hold up with the test?'

'Nope. The test said he was lying both times. Those little spikes couldn't have been any higher. Looked like a couple of mountains on a flat landscape.'

'What did his wife say about his alibi.'

'She backed his story, naturally – tried to protect him. Ross, called her up. She is due to come in in the morning to make a formal statement. Makes no difference- we have enough to hold him until we can get a judge to approve a warrant.'

'It'll still be hard to make it fly in court.' Leighton said. 'His defence will go for unreliability of the lie detector and try to free him on lack of evidence.'

'Maybe, but when put it alongside the neighbour's statement that his car was missing, and the shoe prints.'

'Shoe prints?'

'Yeah we made some footprint casts at both sites. The one from the lagoon is was just a partial – owing to all the footfall, but the

Windmilll Lake ones are pretty clear. They match a shoe type and size owned by Brookes.'

Leighton nodded. 'Sounds like something. I also gave the captain a copy of a statement from Nichols stating that Brookes was bragging about getting into Kelly Coomb's pants.'

'I saw that in the file, good work.'

'So has Brookes been charged?' Leighton asked.

'Not yet,' Daniels said with a wide grin, 'I'm just letting him stew for a while, but if the judge accepts our probable cause and we can get those sneakers from his home, we'll be to make it official. So yeah, it looks like it's in the bag.'

'Good work yourself.' Leighton said and looked back down at his hands.

'Thanks,' Daniels said and turned to go, then paused and leaned back in.

'Hey, Leighton,' Daniels said quietly.

Leighton glanced up surprised to find the detective was back in the doorway. 'Yeah?'

'I just wanted to say, that I've shared the locker-room with Alice for near enough twenty years.' He smiled and seemed lost in the past for a moment. 'You know it seems even longer when you sat it out loud. Anyway, you'll know that she's a lady who always tells it straight.'

'Yep, she sure does,' Leighton said with a warm smile.

'Well,' Daniels rubbed the back of his neck for a moment, 'as far as I can remember- in all that time, you're the only partner that I ever heard her say she liked.'

'Man that's good to hear,' Leighton said.

'Yeah, I just figured you should know.' Daniels said and then left – this time for good.

After Daniels had left to go work on the affidavit and Leighton was alone in the teaching room, he wandered over to the door and locked it. He then returned to continue picking up pencils from the desks. However, after a moment, a wave of sadness washed over him like a dark tide. He gripped a table edge then sat down in a hard plastic chair, staring at the floor and lost in memories.

## 45

The following day, Leighton spent the morning supervising a stretch of dangerous highway just north of the city. Being on his own meant he was kept busy, responding to two breakdowns and then a truck which had a blow-out at sixty miles-per hour.

He returned to the station at lunchtime, partly because he needed to pick up some fresh supplies of road flares, but mainly because he would rather spend twenty minutes of his lunch break driving back to Mission Avenue than sitting alone in the cruiser missing Alice's company.

He had just used the bathroom and was passing by dispatch, when Maria Hernandez who was on the radio called to him.

'Hey Leighton, did you hear?'

'Hear what?' He felt a momentary surge of adrenaline as he half expected to hear that Alice was awake.

'They charged that guy.'

'Brookes?'

'Yeah, Daniels is a happy man – for once. He even said the beers were on him tonight at The Rooster.'

'Has he punched out yet?'

'I don't think so. He's probably still at his desk.'

'Thanks for letting me know.'

'Anytime,' Maria said and put her headset back on again.

Leighton passed through the general office space to a large room at the back, which was shared by Homicide and Vice. Jim Daniels was seated near the back with his jacket over the back of his chair.

'Hey,' Leighton called over to him. 'I hear somebody was charged.'

'Damn true,' Daniels said with a wide smile.

'How did he take it?'

'Well, he called me a dumb-fuck and said his lawyer would tear me a new one.'

'So pretty well then?'

'Exactly,'

'So where is Brookes now?'

'Transferred to MCC this morning. And get this- Brookes didn't want his Rolex and wallet going into the prison stores. Said they would both most likely go missing from there.'

'A killer with trust issues,' Leighton laughed. 'So we getting to pawn his stuff for the station Christmas party?'

'Unfortunately not. His wife is coming to collect his bag of personal belongings from reception later this afternoon.'

'Ah sadly I won't be around to say hi; I'm heading back out on to the busy highway for a couple of hours.'

'You got someone working with you?'

'No, I'm okay on my own.'

'You sure?'

'Yeah, it won't be forever hopefully.'

Daniels nodded but didn't say anything.

46

Lina Brookes red heels clicked of the floor tiles as she approached the reception desk of Oceanside police, with little energy.  The officer on desk duty was Jodie Duncan. Although she was doubtful about the level of her husband's innocence, Jodie was naturally empathic and could see that Lina Brookes was barely managing to keep it all together.

'Hi,' Jodie said softly. 'are you okay?'

Lina nodded and wiped her nose with a crumpled piece of tissue paper. 'I was asked to come in and make some sort of statement and collect my husband's things. Some of your people came round last night to pick up Steve's sneakers – God knows why- but apparently they couldn't drop off his stuff to me.'

'I'm sorry about that.' Jodie said with a warm smile. 'I can get your husband's possessions and arrange for you to sign for them.' She glanced at the desk diary. 'It says here you have a witness statement to sign too. Do you want to take a seat and I'll sort all of this out for you?'

'Can I see him? I'd like to speak to him,' Lina asked bluntly.

'No, that's not possible; Mr Brookes isn't here. Didn't they tell you? This building is just a holding station. After somebody is charged, they are transferred to the MCC in San Diego.'

'Charged? But he hasn't done anything.'

'I really don't know the details. But detective Daniels must've had some reasons.'

'But that night – the one they asked me about, Steve was in the house all night. I said so in my statement.'

'Well, when it goes to court you will get a chance to tell your story.'

Lina nodded but remained standing at the desk. She looked haunted like someone who had just walked out of a disaster area.

'Look, I know this must be really tough for you just now.' Jodie said. 'After you have made your statement, we can arrange for somebody to speak to – explain the whole process, or is there somebody else you would like me to call, a friend or relative perhaps?'

For a moment, Lina said nothing; she simply stared at the tiled floor as if hoping to find some speck of sanity. From somewhere nearby, the noise of a police siren swelled into a wail then faded as a cruiser left the station. The sound seemed to break whatever spell had silenced Lina.

'He's the only man I ever loved. We never had any kids —or friends. It was only ever about us,' she said quietly, as if to herself. 'And I know being locked up will kill him so what the hell am I supposed to do now?'

Jodie, had little to offer the broken woman, but then she realised she could perhaps tell her something. 'Listen, I was on the afternoon shift yesterday, before your husband was transferred. I took his lunch down to him in the holding cells.'

'You did?' Lina asked she seemed suddenly like somebody who had been snapped out of a trance. 'How was he?'

'He really seemed like he was doing okay.' Jodie said with a smile. 'He was even laughing and joking a little.'

'He was?' Lina's eyes widened in disbelief. 'Joking, are you sure?'

'Yeah, honestly. He asked me to sit with him, and said the food here was better than stuff he gets at college. And that was just last night, so maybe you don't need to worry so much.'

'No, maybe I don't,' Lina said with an assertive nod of her head.

'Okay, let me get your husband's items from the store. 'It won't take a minute; I just need to sign a couple of release forms.'

'You take your time,' Lina said.

When the officer returned to the desk, holding with a clear plastic bag containing Brookes' belongings, she found that Lina had gone.

'I'll be damned,' Jodie said and shook her head.

## 47

Corey Troy burst through a fire door at the rear of the college swimming pool, and then hurried down a flight of stairs which led to a small parking lot, which was mainly used by janitorial staff. He snaked between a couple of catering supplies trucks, and then crossed a wide lawn and headed to a secluded area where a two wooden picnic tables were located.

After sitting down at one of the tables, Troy pulled a pack of Marlboro cigarettes from his shirt. He took a cigarette from the pack and lit it with trembling hands- one of which was bleeding. Frowning, Troy blew out a cone of smoke, then rubbed vigorously at the edges of the injury, causing small crumbs of dried blood to fall onto the legs of his bleached jeans like rust.

The anger he felt was bubbling in him like acid, and he knew that it would was getting to the point of being impossible to ignore.

Violent fantasies swam through his head like swirling shades of crimson, yet he knew that acting upon any of them would place him in jail. And yet the urge was difficult to resist. He felt like he was drowning in emotion.

Troy turned his head, glancing over his shoulder for a moment before reaching the bloodied hand into the collar of his t-shirt and then pulled out the ID badge hung attached to the red lanyard. He held up Kelly's pass in front of his face and felt a surge of pain so raw it was almost physical.

## 47

It was late in the afternoon when Jodie Duncan finished her shift. She had got held up on an endless phone call from a concerned member of the public – complaining about teenagers dealing drugs down by the skate park, and demanding that something be done about it. Eventually, with her ear still warm from being pressed against the handset, Jodie walked through the small corridor which led to the locker area. Mounted on one wall there was a booking systems of cards held in vertical slots indicating which officers were on duty. She deftly shifted her own card from on to off duty, and then walked through to the locker room.

Jodie whistled cheerfully as she changed into a pair of grey sweatpants and a peach-coloured t-shirt. Most days she would drive home in her uniform but tonight she planned to hit the gym for an hour with – Danni Marquez- one of the young female officers who worked in Community Policing.

She left the station building and crossed the hot parking lot to where her Fiat was parked. A foil sunscreen covered the windshield. Jodie had invested in this to stop the black plastic seats from becoming blistering hot beneath the Californian sun.

After climbing into her car, Jodie reached across to the glove box where she kept her sunglasses. The frames were cheap metal and didn't warrant a protective case, however if they too were affected by the heat and if Jodie left them in the sunshine they would scorch the top of her ears. She put her glasses on then started the car engine. The sound of Billy Idol singing White Wedding filled the car. Singing along loudly with the music, Jodie put her car in gear and drove out of the station parking lot.

An hour later, Jodie lay curled in the dark womb of a car trunk.

## 48

Leighton wandered back into the station at 6.12 pm. There was no reason to hurry home, and he knew that he could stop by the hospital to visit Alice. However, his plans changed when he entered the building and met Detective Ross in the deserted corridor leading from the lockers to the office areas.

'Hey Jones, how you doin?' Ross asked.

'Good,' Leighton lied. 'It's a little quiet in here this afternoon. What's going on?'

'Yeah, it's the formal launch of the Californian Antidrug Initiative at Mira Costa College, most of the crew are there. Dispatch, and the night desk are the only areas being covered in here, but the patrols are all fully staffed, so at least the streets will be safe.'

'Shit!' was I meant to be there?'

'It's okay, Alice had originally signed you both up for it but after… well, the captain asked Tom Feltz and Ray Gratten to go. Plus, you've had enough shit to deal with.'

'Yeah, I have bene a bit preoccupied, but it was worth when heard you guys had caught Brookes out.'

'Yeah, he's one slippery bastard.'

'No doubt he will be busy getting himself all lawyered up.'

'Might not do him any good. Daniels is in the process of submitting an affidavit for a warrant to access his home and office tomorrow morning. Chances are he'll get it too.'

'What about his wife? Daniels said she tried to give Brookes and alibi.'

'She'll be brought in for an interview whilst the forensic team are going over the house. We'll see how well her alibi holds up under formal questioning.'

'Daniels said that she was meant to come over today, did she show?'

Yeah, but that was the damnedest thing...;

'What was?'

'Well, apparently the wife showed up in reception this afternoon to collect Brookes' personal belongings, but for some reason she just left without them – just walked away.'

'Pretty weird.' Leighton said. 'Did she talk to anyone, say anything?'

'I've not heard. Jodie Duncan was working reception, but she clocked off at 4.pm. You could check with her tomorrow – see what was said.'

'Sure, I think I will,' Leighton replied.

'Anyway,' Ross shrugged, 'it's pretty much over now.'

After Ross had gone home, Leighton. Went through to his desk and sat down. He ran one hand over his face. He had been telling the truth when he told Ross how he felt it was all worthwhile knowing that Brookes was in jail. However, there were still some things that bothered Leighton. The Salton Sea thing was still playing on his mind. He couldn't figure out why the Brookes would even want to live out there in the middle of nowhere, which was miles from any college. Unless that was somehow his intention.

He picked up the telephone handset and rested it between his ear and shoulder as he opened a drawer and pulled out a telephone directory. He flipped through page after page until he reached Colleges and universities. Eventually, he found the one he was looking for and ran the tip of his index finger down the page. He stopped with his fingernail resting on one of the institutions. Keeping one hand on the directory, he used the other one to dial the number.

As the phone rang at the other end, Leighton grew increasingly doubtful that anyone would still be around to answer his call and he would be redirected to answer-machine.

However, after a few moments. There was a click and a thankfully real person spoke.

'William Jessops University, how may I help you?'

'Hi there, my name is officer Leighton Jones of Oceanside PD. I was wondering if you could answer a couple of questions for me.'

After almost an hour on the telephone, Leighton thanked the administrator and hung up. He had a much fuller picture of events, and wanted to share his findings with Ross and Daniels the following morning, but was worried that he might not see them before they began interviewing Mrs Brookes. He had filled almost an entire page with notes, which he tore from the pad and carried with as he stood up and walked through to the Homicide area.

This office space was dominated by three large felt covered pinboards, which served as a way to organise evidence, along with victim and suspect profiles. The first two boards were devoted to four shootings believed to be related to drug dealing near Camp Pendleton. However, the third and smaller board featured images and information relating to Brookes and his activities.

Leighton passed by the boards as he made his way to Jim Daniels area. As he placed the sheet of notes on the desk, Leighton smiled at the plastic framed photograph of a much younger Daniels fresh from the academy standing grinning outside the station entrance. Leighton wondered how much Daniels had changed since the picture was taken. A whole lot, he imagined. He was glad that he and Daniels had made their peace. Alice would be proud of her rookie for that, though she might not tell him.

As Leighton turned and walked back out of the office he glanced over at the final display board. There was an image of Brookes, which looked like it had been taken from his driver's license. He was younger and wearing tinted glasses, but the confidence he exuded was still there. However, it was not this photograph which caught Leighton's eye; it was the two photographs beneath it. The images featuring Kelly Coombs and Sarah Levin. Both girls were smiling and looked achingly full of life. Having the two images side by side highlighted the similarity between the two. Then Leighton noticed a third smaller photograph of to one side with a question mark next to it. This picture was a highs school yearbook photograph of Amy-lee (NAME) showed another similar looking girl who easily looked as if she could be a younger sister of the other two. It had to be true. She must've been another one of his victims.

Leighton mouthed a silent prayer for the three victims and then was just about to leave when he realised something. The three girls in the photographs reminded him of someone. For a moment he frowned in concentration, thinking it might be a popstar or actress, but then he remembered exactly who it was.

At that moment, officer Adam Elmwood – who had been working reception- walked in and mentioned the person he was thinking of.

'Hey Jonesy, I just had (Name) call in. She was due to meet Jodie Duncan at the gym tonight but she never showed, so she took a drive by her apartment and it's deathly quiet. (Name) was wondering if she might still be here.'

'Oh shit!' Leighton shouted and ran out of the office. 'Send a unit to the Brookes' place on Cardiff Bay Drive.'

49

Leighton pulled up his car just outside the Brookes family home. After being trapped in crawling traffic roadworks on Douglas Drive for half an hour, he was relieved to see cars in the driveway. He got of the vehicle and glanced at the building. The wooden shutters were all closed. Leighton walked cautiously up the driveway where both cars were parked side by side facing the garage doors.

It was only by chance that he glanced inside the two cars and confirmed his suspicions. Steve's red Lancia was unchanged from when he had seen it last. However, it was as he glanced at the smaller white car that Leighton noticed the rear view mirror. It had been twisted all the way round.

Leighton's demeanour suddenly shifted. Unclipped his holster and then slowly slid his hand over the grip of his revolver.

He stepped forward and knocked on the door

'Mrs Brookes, my name is Leighton Jones, I'm a police officer.'

'Step back from the door!'

'Okay, I'm doing it now Leighton said with his hand raised. 'I just want to speak to you.'

The door opened and Lina Brookes appeared. Holding a silver pistol in one hand. It was pointed at the police officer's head. Leighton raised his hands in the air.

'You really don't need to do this,' he said softy.

'Shut up and back away until you're standing on the lawn.'

Leighton took four or five steps back wards until the gravel beneath his feet gave way to brittle blades of grass.

Lina kept her eyes and the weapon and Leighton as she approached her car and carefully opened the door.

'Hey, listen- I only came to drop off your husband's things,' Leighton called.

'You're not a very convincing liar.' Lina said. 'Toss your gun over there.' Lina Brookes nodded towards some rose bushes at the side of her home.

'Leighton moved his hand to his holster, but Lina immediately cocked the hammer on hers. 'Slowly,' she said.

Using just his thumb and forefinger, Leighton carefully took his service pistol out of the holster and threw it away.

'Good boy,' Lina said as she walked over to Leighton's cruiser. She glanced in the open driver's window.

'So you're all alone,' she said, 'that's good.' Lina pointed the gun into the car and shot the radio.

Leighton made to step instinctively forward, but Lina was fast and swivelled to point the weapon at him again. 'Don't be stupid, officer.'

She walked back to her own car.

'Where's Jodie?' Leighton called.

'Preparing to meet her maker.' Lina said. She remained focussed on Leighton as she climbed into the driver's seat, leaving the door open, and the handgun pointed straight at him.

'Step a little closer to me please,' Lina said cheerfully.

Leighton moved nearer to the car.

'Stop!' Lina said as Leighton was only a couple of steps from her.

'I just want to know if she's alive?'

'Of course she is, but she soon won't be. But it'll make no difference to you- unless you see her in the afterlife. Now stay still. I'm not a great shot.' She then raised the gun to point at Leighton's face.

'Hey!' a male voice called from the street behind Lina's car. She instinctively glanced over her shoulder for a moment, and in that fraction of a second Leighton suddenly leapt towards her car. He managed to slam the door on Lina's arm, and grabbed the barrel of the pistol in an attempt to direct it downwards. Lina roared in pain and rage and then fired the gun.

There was blinding flash, accompanied by a deafening bang and then a small red cloud appeared momentarily above Leighton's shoe like the smoke of a firecracker. Leighton crumpled to the ground. The weapon used upon him landed beside Leighton on the ground, but he was too distracted to notice. Reaching for his bleeding he foot, he groaned in the grip spiralling agony. He looked up as he heard the roar of the car engine, and then watched in horror as it reversed out of the driveway and screeched away.

## 50

Corey Troy had already committed himself to the act when all hell broke loose.

It had been two weeks since the last shift he had shared with Kelly Coombs. To him, Kelly was perfect. The previous year when they had first started working together had been like a dream come true for Troy who had grown up with three ugly brothers. She seemed like a sculpture of some Greek goddess.

In an attempt to get a chance to talk with her, Troy had started showing up at the pool when Kelly was working even when he didn't have a shift. This meant he couldn't go to the poolside but he would linger around at the start and end of her shift. It was never meant to be sinister, but he could see how it might seem that way. Eventually, he appeared so often that Kelly complained to administration – and they logged it as harassment and asked him to stop – or face being sacked from the job. A far as Corey was concerned, he was horrified. He never intended to frighten or annoy Kelly, yet his attempts to get closer to her had meant he risked never getting to work with her again. That would be unbearable, so he resigned himself to only seeing Kelly during his shifts. He was unwilling to risk losing that. It was difficult only seeing her on those odd days, but it was better than nothing.

But he still ached to see her, and then on their last shift together he Kelly had scurried quickly out of the pool side, accidentally leaving her ID badge and lanyard on her observation seat. That was when Troy had been passing and could not believe his luck. He picked it up, and then wound it around his hand as Claire Steiner- the other pool guard walked over to begin her shift. took it. She was too busy checking the water level to even notice what Troy was holding as her hurried away.

Initially, he had thought he could take the pass back to Kelly and perhaps then she would see that he was a good guy after all. But once he had taken it back to his room, like Gollum with the ring, the ID badge seduced him. It was like having a glowing piece of Kelly with him, in his own grubby world.

Then she vanished and then everything fell apart. Troy wanted to do something, anything to help.

Of course on the day, he saw Kelly with Marc Nicholls, he got it wrong, and when the rumour that Steve Brookes had been arrested spread around the campus, it made much more sense.

Lots of students liked Brookes, but Troy could see him for what he was- a smiling villain. He would stride through the corridors in a cloud of cologne and self-confidence, checking out any young blonde females.

When word reached the campus that Kelly had been found dead, Troy was broken.

He was unable to eat or sleep. He still attended his job at the pool even though- or perhaps because- it was impossible to walk along the pool edge without glancing around expecting to see her there. Even his usual refuge of fantasy fiction could no longer provide any escape. Kelly was all he could think about- her and that sick bastard Steve Brookes. It ran over and over in his mind like a looped movie.

Earlier that week, Corey had heard through the college grapevine that Brookes had been arrested over Kelly's death. As terrible as that confirmation of Troy's suspicions had been, it had also provided a small degree of comfort, in the sense that Brookes was going to be punished. However, this morning Angelina Guerrez who worked the early shift mopping the pool changing-rooms and whose sister was cleaner in Oceanside Police Station-had told Troy that the girl's killer would get a good lawyer and could easily be set free at any moment.

At the end of his shift ran across the campus to Brookes' tutor room, threw open the door and then smashed the place up, punching his fists into the framed certificates and sweeping leather bound books onto the floor. The destruction of Brookes' world just as he had destroyed Troy's had offered some form of release, but it was not enough – it wasn't justice for Kelly.

Breathing hard and, with bruised and bleeding fists he had fled the building. To find a place to think. Eventually as he had sat and smoked on a picnic bench at the back of the campus, that he would call up reception and ask for Brookes' address, claiming that he some expensive borrowed books to return. Then he would go to the bastard's house and wait for his return.

Troy had recognised Leighton as he arrived at property. Thinking that he might be escorting Steve Brookes back home, Troy had sunk down in the warm undergrowth at the side of an adjacent property. He was surprised to discover that the cop was alone, but then as the officer approached the door, Troy figured Brookes may already be inside the house. This possibility caused a ripple of adrenaline to flex through Troy's body, leaving him ready to strike if the bastard opened the door. The situation was one he had rehearsed it a thousand times in his head. He imagined walking up to Brookes and punching and kicking him until he was silent and broken.

But things did not unfold the way Corey had imagined. Firstly, it had been a woman who answered the door rather that freak Brookes, and secondly, the woman had calmly shot the police officer in the foot, before jumping in her car and racing away.

Corey had, felt his heart thumping in his chest as he scrambled out of his hiding place. He wasn't even sure that his legs, which had been numbed by almost an hour spent crouching, would carry him across the street to where the wounded cop lay, but the adrenaline from seeing a shooting close-up was enough to drive him forwards. He reached Leighton as he was attempting unsuccessfully to get on his feet.

'Officer! It's me – Corey Troy. You need to stay there. We need to call an ambulance. '

Leighton looked up, frowning in confusion.

'Why are you here – no, it doesn't matter,' he grunted. 'Help me to my car.'

'Okay,' Corey looked scared, but he did as he was asked and supported Leighton as he grunted to his feet.

As Leighton began hobbling towards the car, he pointed back at the ground. 'Hold on, can you grab that pistol, and the one under the bushes.'

Corey looked at Leighton. 'Can you stand?' he asked.

'Sure, just hurry.'

Troy hesitantly left Leighton swaying unsteadily, and scrambled around to grab the two weapons. He then hurried back to Leighton, looking like a boyish wild-west gunslinger with a pistol in each hand.

'Watch where you point those things,' Leighton said. 'Right, let's get in the car. Can you drive?'

'Sure,' Troy said. 'Never driven a cop car though.'

'Don't worry,' Leighton said breathlessly as he reached the vehicle, 'the steering wheel is the pretty much the same shape. Let's go.'

51

As she awoke in the hot airless darkness of her prison, Jodie Duncan's head was pounding and for a moment she struggled to understand what had happened. Initially, she thought she may have been an automobile accident and was trapped in the wreckage, but then she realised it was much worse than that.

Turning her aching head to one side, Jodie felt a sudden pain as her hair, matted with blood, tore away from the carpet it had been fused to.

She could remember driving back from work, and pulling up in the small parking lot outside her apartment and was vaguely aware of a car pulling up behind her.

Whoever had abducted her must have hit her from behind as she pushed the key into the lock of her apartment. After that they had bound her hands and feet and placed her inside the baking hot trunk of a car. A piece of duct tape had been wrapped around Jodie's mouth and head so tightly that she could taste blood form where her lips crushed against her teeth. Writhing from side to side she tried to kick at the walls of her sweltering coffin but there was little room to move...

## 52

'You know she could be miles away,' Troy said as he pulled the car away from the house.

'No she won't be,' Leighton said, 'There are heavy roadworks all along Douglas Drive. It's down to one lane. She'll be hopefully be stuck in it.'

As Troy pulled out of the residential area and on to the long dusty road of Douglas Drive, he discovered that Leighton had been correct. The two lanes had been reduced down to one, with an endless row of road cones on one side, and an unbroken fence on the other. These two barriers formed a two-mile channel in which the cars were crawling down towards the city.

'Should we use the sirens? Try to clear some space.' Troy asked.

'No point' Leighton grunted. 'There's nowhere for the cars in front to go. It flattens out up ahead. Plus, I don't want her to know we are here just yet – oh shit, too late! She's moving.'

Suddenly, Lina's car broke out of the lane of vehicles and crashed through the fence, which separated the road from the arid hillside. There was a cloud of dust swirling behind the car as it bounced away from the traffic.

'What do I do?' Troy screeched.

'Follow her!' Leighton shouted and then screamed in pain as he instinctively pressed with his accelerator foot.

While Leighton reached to the dash and flicked a switch causing the sirens to wail. Troy twisted the steering wheel and the cruiser lurched to the side. There was a squeal of metal as the car pushed through the metal barrier and into the scrubland.

The car shuddered as it cut through the bushes and shrubs edging the road. For a moment Leighton thought they had lost the silver car. But then he noticed a plume of dust above the dense bushes further ahead. 'She's up there,' he said pointing the direction Troy should take.

'This is one long valley so stick to the higher ground. Otherwise we might end upside down in a creek.'

Troy nodded and gripped the wheel a little more tightly as he drove into the wilderness.

The cruiser followed the car for almost a half a mile through the dry undergrowth, before it finally burst back into civilisation and onto a ramp for Highway 76. As Lina veered into the traffic a large orchard truck had to swerve to avoid hitting her.

With the roadworks and associated traffic were thankfully far behind, Leighton reached down and tried swivelling the dial on the damaged radio. There was crackling noise but nothing more. He lifted the handset to his mouth. 'Dispatch this is Adam 322. I don't know it you can hear me. I am in pursuit of a silver (Name) heading west on 76. Requesting immediate back up.

Troy and Leighton followed the silver car as it drove into the harbour area passing by the rows of glossy white boats in the marina, to end up in large parking lot.

'She's running out or road,' Troy said hopefully.

'That's what she wants,' Leighton said. 'Can you swim?'

'What?'

'Can you swim – if she drives into the sea?'

Troy blinked as he struggled to comprehend. 'Why would she-'

'Look!' Leighton pointed up ahead to where Lina had driven her car over the edge of the parking lot forcing its way through large rocks place there as a barrier. The car trundled along and towards the water and then stopped on an old slipway. The front of the car was facing the water.

Troy pulled over at the sand covered end of the parking area.

'You want me to go any closer?' he asked.

'No. Stay here! You did real good.' Leighton said.

'But, I still want to help.'

'Then keep twisting the dial on that radio. If you get anybody speaking on it, tell them we're at the harbour just beyond tower 16. And keep your head down. For all we know, she might be carrying a second weapon.'

Leighton groaned in pain as he got out of the car. He held his pistol tightly as he approached. As he limped towards the silver car, he noticed that there wasn't any smoke coming out of the exhaust pipe. That was a good sign. If she had Jodie in the trunk, and decided to drive a full speed into the waves, he would have no chance of stopping it.

The car window was down and Lina Brookes was staring straight ahead. Her hands remained on the steering wheel as if glued there.

'Where's Jodie, Lina?'

Lina swivelled her head to look at Leighton and then returned her gaze to the tumbling waves. 'That horny little bitch will learn a tough lesson.'

'So, where is she?'

'Sorry, officer - a woman must have her secrets.'

'She never did anything to you?'

Lina turned instantly back to look at Leighton. Her face was contorted with rage. 'No, nothing at all – except try to steal my husband.'

'Is that what you believed Kelly Coombs was doing – is that why you killed her?'

'Move on,' Lina said with a shrug, 'Nobody cares about that little slut either.'

'I do,' Leighton said firmly.

'Yeah well maybe you like them young and dumb too.'

'Just like Steve does?' Leighton knew this might light the touch paper.

'Fuck you!' Lina's eyes burned with hot rage.

'Why did you choose the lagoon?'

'You tell me?'

'I think you figured that dumping the girls in the lagoon and the waste water pond would make retrieving evidence from them difficult.'

Lina laughed. It was a cold sound. 'How would I come up with something like that?'

'Well, you studied Aqua-culture at college didn't you?'

Lina stopped smiling.

'I am a cop, so I did a little digging and found out that you were called Lina Warren and that you completed two years of study in the marine sciences faculty over at William Jessop… until you had to leave.'

'Maybe- that was thirteen years ago. I really don't remember.'

Leighton tried a different route. 'Is that when you met Steve?'

'Yeah, so what? She said then smiled at some private memory. 'He couldn't keep away from me.'

'He was a lecturer at that time?'

'He wasn't my lecturer – but he taught me so much.' Lina winked.

'The way I heard it, you got kicked out of college after getting caught screwing him in a store-cupboard. So, essentially the relationships cost you your education.'

'Well, it was worth it just to be with him. Everyone could see that we were meant for each other – and we've been together for thirteen perfect years.'

'Until Steve began to show an interest in other girls?'

Leighton's words triggered a sudden shift in Lina's expression

'That's not true – it was those bitches who were interested in him Steve didn't want the attention.'

'No?'

'They pursued him – like horny little dogs – fluttering their pretty fuckin eyelashes at him.'

Leighton could feel the sudden rage emanating from the woman like a white heat. He decided to capitalise on it

'That must've been hard on you.' Leighton deliberately softened his expression to show concern.

'You don't know the half of it – phone calls, notes in his pocket. 'He tried to put them off, but they just kept coming at him like flies.'

'Like your neighbour Amy-lee?'

'She drowned her swimming pool. Case closed.'

'I think maybe Steve took an interest in her. Am I right?'

'She didn't even know him, until that idiot offered to tutor her for her high school History course. I mean he must have known what would happen.'

'What did happen?'

'I told you already, she got drunk one night when her parents were away overnight at a show in Reno. Somehow, she ended up in the water.'

'But you reckon she was interested in Steve, just like Kelly Coombs was?'

'Hell yes. That's exactly what I'm talking about.'

'Tell me about her,' Leighton was trying to play for time, hoping that backup would arrive and he wouldn't have to figure this out by himself, but his lower leg was becoming increasingly numb.

Lina Brookes, however, was smiling vaguely as she recalled some past memory.

'When we first met, Steve used to tell me that my eyes were beautiful and sparkling; like sapphires in the snow. in recent years he stopped saying it. I guess those little prick-teases had nicer eyes than mine.'

'Is that why you do that?' Leighton nodded towards the twisted mirror.

'Maybe,' Lina said with an unconvincing attempt at an indifferent shrug. She then stared out towards the ocean waves and seem lost in her recollections. Eventually, she spoke.

'I suspected something was wrong for a couple of weeks. Steve was quiet, not interested in touching me and he had stopped eating. Then, as always, he couldn't stop himself from saying her name – it would spill out of him, punctuating his conversation like a confession – like he wanted me to know.'

'So what did you do?'

'I paid the guy who mows the lawn twenty dollars to call up each of the residences and asked if they had a student by that name.'

'And he did it?'

'Yeah, I told him that I had found a purse with that name and U of SD printed inside but I was too shy to call myself. So, I took the telephone out to the garden and poured him a cold beer whilst he worked through the calls.'

'Then what happened?'

'It wasn't like you imagine – I was planning to take a drive over there just to tell the girl to keep her hands off my husband, but then something happened.'

'Something?'

'I was out for at an exercise class down at Donnie's Gym on the boulevard, but I felt sick halfway through – I think perhaps it was my woman's intuition. So I drove home early and discovered the little bitch's car was parked in our driveway.

'Did you confront her?'

'No. I drove over to her residences and wrote a note for her – from Steve.'

'A note saying what?'

'That my husband wanted to meet her. I said he wanted to talk about them running away together.'

'Where did you agree to meet?'

'Down at the lagoon. After I left the note, I went down to the lagoon and started drinking bourbon straight out of the bottle.'

'You wore his sneakers, why?'

'We were in this together. If I was going to get caught, I wanted him implicated too.'

'How did you know that Kelly would turn up?'

'If I was her I would have. Steve has that ability to cast a spell over women. They would do anything to be with him.'

'What happened when she showed up?'

'I hit her from behind with a rock, put her back in the driver's seat, and then took off the parking brake and let it roll into the water. Figured it might look like suicide.'

'But she got out, didn't she?' Leighton suddenly understood the two deep lines he had seen in the sand.

'Hell, that little bitch swam to the side like a fucking mermaid. I was just getting back into my own car when I saw her crawling out of the water on her hands and knees.'

'What did you do?'

'I walked over to her. She was all bent over spluttering and choking. So I took my chance and hit her again, with my tyre iron this time. But by then it was too late; her car was already under the water.'

'So you were stuck with a body?' Leighton tried to make it sound perfectly normal.

'Exactly!'

'So what did you do?'

'I dragged her over to my car and dumped her in the trunk. I wasn't thinking; I just wanted to get out of there.'

'Where did you go?' Leighton asked, though he knew the answer to the question.

'I drove up on to the road over the beach and realised I couldn't go home with a dead girl in the trunk, so I pulled over on the boulevard, dragged her out of the trunk and tossed the little bitch over the railings.'

'And no-one saw you?'

'It was dark, but if they did, they didn't do anything about it.

'But she wasn't the first one, was she?'

'What makes you say that?'

'I just reckon you seem a little to calm for someone who has just killed for the first time. Most people would fall apart.'

'Well, you are quite the boy scout aren't you? I told you the neighbour's kid drowned.'

'I'm not talking about Amy-lee. What happened to Sarah Levin?'

'You tell me?'

'I think you may have seen Steve in the coffee shop. He was talking to an attractive young woman who was serving him coffee. Maybe they were smiling at each other – sitting together maybe- and so you figured she liked him.'

Lina said nothing. Perhaps she felt she was knee deep in shit already and so should maybe stop wading. Leighton decided to push her buttons. 'Or maybe you figured he liked her?'

A darkness crossed the woman's face but she remained silent.

'How did you manage to get her up to Windmill Lake?'

It seemed like Lina would remain sitting in silence, but something changed in her expression and she seemed suddenly transfixed by some memory and she spoke as if in the darkness of a dream.

'Steve wouldn't stop mentioning her fucking name. I told you, that's how I would know when one of them had put a spell on him and wormed under his fucking skin. It was like I wasn't even there when he spoke about her. *Poor Sarah at the coffee shop,* was all I ever heard. He seemed convinced that she had some tragic story with a momma in jail and he went on and on about how she didn't even have a high school diploma. Steve told me he figured he could help her- maybe arrange to tutor her – help her to get on to her feet. I knew what she was up to. She had worked in him so long with her big eyes, that now he wanted to get into her pants, it was so fucking obvious. Steve didn't stand a chance.' Lina nodded proudly to herself.

'So you figured it out?'

'Exactly.' Lina sounded proud.

'What did you do?'

'I stopped in at the cafe when Steve was at work- left an envelope with the little slut's name on it. It was an invitation from Steve to run away together. It's amazing how the thought of stealing another woman's husband can make some dumb bitch pack up her life and drive to the middle of fucking nowhere at midnight.'

'How did you get her into the water?'

'The note said to come to the edge of the smaller lake because that area couldn't be seen from the road or nearby buildings. So I drove over there and parked up behind the buildings.

I walked to the edge of the water and waited in the darkness.'

'How long were you there, waiting?'

'An hour maybe, but it's so dark out there away from all the lights. I could see so many stars. It was crazy. Then eventually I noticed the lights of a car winding its way up from town towards the me.'

'How did you feel?'

'I was full of hate and cruelty, so I felt ready to do what I needed to, I suppose.'

'So what happened?'

'When the girl arrived, she got out of the car to look around. I climbed into the back seat and waited. It stank of her perfume. Little bitch must've wanted to smell sweet for him.'

'So what happened?'

'When she eventually got cold or bored, she got back into the car and I sat up and slammed her head against the steering wheel. After that I put the car in the water- that one at least stayed inside.'

Leighton tried to push the thought of the girl's final moments away, but his own anger was difficult to contain.

'So did that make you feel secure again – did it fix things for you?'

'Well, it did until Steve caught the eye of that bitch in heat at the police station.'

'Jodie has no interest in your husband.'

'What would you know?' Lina scoffed. 'She said he was sweet — that' she had to take care of him. We both know what that meant. It wouldn't be long before she was grinding down on him on a bed in some shitty little motel.'

'You're wrong.'

'I doubt someone like you could understand.'

'Like me?'

'Yeah, bland, ugly and dumb. I doubt any woman has shown interest in you, let alone wanted to be with you like they do with men like my Steve.'

'Yeah, that's probably true, but you can end this. Just tell me where Jodie is.'

'Are you thinking of arresting me?'

'Yes, I am.'

'Then I suppose I will be going to jail.'

'Probably.' Leighton tried to say the word casually – attempting to conceal his certainty that Mrs Brookes would spend the next twenty years in jail.

'Then, if that happens, Steve will be free and that little bitch will come sniffing around him again. Don't you see? That's why I can't let you have her. You asked me why I chose to put them in the water.'

'Yeah, I did.'

'It's nothing to do with evidence – I never even thought about evidence – at least not consciously.'

'Then why did you put them in the water?'

'When I was a kid in Reno, my dad taught History in the local high school, so we had all these old text books lying around the house. I wasn't interested in looking at any of them. Most were about Colonial politics and economics in, pretty boring - except for one. It was about witch trials.'

'Salem?'

'No, it was more about what happened in Europe. When a woman was suspected of being a witch, she would have a trial by water. They would tie a rope around her and throw her in a river or lake. If she was pure, the water would take her life.'

'And if it didn't?'

'She was a witch- a sinner- they all were. And so they deserved a trial by water?'

'I don't believe in witches, Mrs Brookes. I think those people accused were poor women, judged by others who were fearful or jealous of them. Like four girls you murdered.'

'Four?'

'Oh yes, we know about Ellie Johnstone out a Salton City. Did Steve like her too?'

'Never heard of her,' Lina said with a dismissive shrug.

'Just another unimportant life, huh?'

'The way I see it, if the girls hanging around my husband had been pure, God would have intervened and saved them.'

'But you already told me Kelly did survive the water, yet you killed her anyway.'

'Well, I guess you got me on that one. But we all make choices. Steve is no better- he couldn't stay away from them – even in death. He even kept a little box of trinkets hidden in our bedroom.'

'You think he is worse?'

'He chose their fate.'

'No, you did! And you're going to face justice for the murder of these young women.'

'Maybe, but maybe not. It will really depend on whether you choose to save the slut in the back of my car or not.'

'What do you mean?'

'Well, I imagine that you wanted to keep me talking, give the other cops time to show up, right? Probably made you feel in charge, like a real little lawman. But here's the thing – it was me who wanted to keep you talking.'

'I don't understand,' Leighton felt as if he had been slapped.

The tide has come in far enough to cover that little bitch in the trunk.

Leighton looked in horror towards the rear of the vehicle.

'So' Lina continued cheerfully, 'she too can still have her trial by water.'

Whilst Leighton shifted his attention towards the trunk, Lina flung her car door open, and leapt out, slamming into Leighton. He stumbled backwards on the uneven sand, and screamed in pain as he placed all his weight on his wounded foot. As he struggled to regain his balance, Leighton watched in horror as Lina's car began to roll slowly into the ocean waves. Scrambling towards the vehicle, he felt a froth of salt water cover his shoe and wash into the open wound in his foot. Behind him, Lina Brookes was already stumbling along the beach, escaping the chaos she had created.

Leighton managed to pull on the parking break just as the fender and front wheels vanished beneath the water.

'Troy!' Leighton yelled, but there was no need; the young man was already out of the cruiser and running towards him.

'Stop! She's in the trunk!' Leighton called. 'Go back and grab the tyre iron from my car. We should be able to prise it open.'

'Sure, okay,' Troy nodded, and turned back around.

As the silver car rolled into the water, Leighton managed to open the driver door for a couple of inches, but the force of the water pushing against the side of the car was too strong to resist.

'Got it!'

Leighton turned to see Troy running towards him with the tyre iron held aloft like an Olympian.

'Get to the trunk!' Leighton called. 'We need to see if we can prise it.

Limping to the rear of the vehicle as it crept forward, Leighton joined Troy. 'Jam it in above the lock, otherwise the metal will just move but it still won't open.'

Troy did as he was told, and slotted the narrow end of the tyre iron into the narrow gap between the lid of the trunk and the body of the car. '

Both men pushed down on the metal bar and levered it. There was a groan of metal and then finally the trunk sprang open with a metallic clunk.

The young woman curled inside the cramped space was tied and up, her mouth was taped. missing a shoe and had a purple bruise on her forehead.

'Is she alive?' Troy asked.

Leighton leaned into the cavity and gently placed his index and middle fingers on the side of the female officer's neck. For a moment, he thought she was dead, but then he shifted his fingers and found the slow, steady pulse. Troy watched in fascination. It seemed as if he had tumbled through a trapdoor of everyday life into one of his books.

'She's got a pulse. Help me get her out of there.'

Troy helped Leighton to clumsily lift Jodie from the boot and place her on the rear seat of the cruiser. He produced a small pocket knife and began cutting through her bindings.

'You did well Corey, but I'll need you to drive us all to the hospital, it'll be faster than waiting for an ambulance to be dispatched. I just need to radio the station and let dispatch know that Lina Brookes escaped on foot.'

'Actually, Mr Jones, I don't think she did.' Troy was holding on to open door and staring over Leighton's shoulder.

Leighton looked up to meet Troy's gaze, but he realised that the young man's eyes were fixed on a distant point on the horizon. Turning slowly, Leighton followed the direction in which Troy was looking and his eyes widened in surprise.

## 53

Less than a quarter of a mile from the location of the cruiser, the beach changed in gradient from steep to shallow. Despite this, there were no beach huts or loungers; there were only regular signs warning of the particular beach hazards linked to the area. The sand at this point on faded from a pale ivory colour to a darker caramel tone, which stretched out the distant tide. It was here, in this strip of darkness, that something was moving frantically. Initially, Leighton thought he was looking at what might be a large bird caught in some abandoned netting. However, as his eyes adjusted, Leighton realised he was looking at the upper torso of a woman sticking out of the sand, her arms flailing as if waving to some distant friend.

'What's happened to her?' Troy asked.

'The run off from the hurricane must've destabilised the sands around here. If you walk on it, each step takes you deeper in until there is nothing to stand on. It happened last season too. A woman got stuck, then so did the fire crew sent to rescue her.'

'How do we get her out?'

For a moment, Leighton said nothing. Troy realised that he was possibly considering whether they even should.

'Carefully,' Leighton said finally.'

'I'm pretty light,' Troy said, 'I should be okay.'

Leighton glanced at him. 'I'm not talking about the sand.'

'Oh.' Troy nodded.

Leighton leaned into his car and called for an ambulance and back up to apprehend a murder suspect. He then grunted as he limped to the trunk of his car and removed a coil of orange rope.

'Come on, we haven't much time.'

As Leighton and Troy approached the strip of dark sand, between the ocean and beach, in which Lina Brookes was sinking, they were both faced with a bizarre scene. The woman looked like a someone taking a frantic swim a pool of wet sand. She had sunk up to her chest and was holding her arms out as if to start some aquatic exercise class, but it was clear that each movement was contributing to the suction from the slurry all around her. Every few seconds, she would make tentative move forwards, only to sink half an inch deeper into the sandy liquid. By the time the two men were close enough to speak with her, Lina Brookes had sunk up to her shoulders. Despite this, she looked like somebody not fully aware of the danger of their situation.

'How you doing, Mrs Brookes?' Leighton called to her. 'Quite the escape you made there.'

'Fuck you!' Lina called angrily from her sandy prison.

Leighton winced as he lowered himself on to the sand. He then stepped carefully near to where Lina Brookes was stuck like a floundering fish.

'I imagine that by now you're finding it a little hard to breathe!' he shouted. 'All that heavy wet sand must be crushing the life right out of you. In fact, it must feel a little like Sarah Levin must've felt up at Windmill Lake. I mean, I suspect you don't want to think about that, do you? But, I'd like you to – imagine being confused as you wake up to find that you're stuck in a car sinking in cold, dark water. I want you to think about what those final moments must've been like.'

'You are indulging yourself with fucked up fantasies - they were all dead when they went into the water!' Lina Brookes called.

'Not according to the coroner,' Leighton said. 'Sarah tore of two finger nails trying to take off her seatbelt as the water filled her car. But, I guess that in a few minutes you won't need to imagine; you can experience it first-hand.'

The woman began to shift, around but her movement only caused her to sink a little deeper.

For a moment, Leighton could only watch as the expression on Lina Brookes' face change from defiance to fear.

Then, as the steady rise and fall of approaching sirens filled the warm evening air, Leighton looped one end of the rope around his arm then threw rest to Lina Brookes. For a moment she only looked at the rope, but did not actually reach for it.

'I don't mind if you don't want to take it!' Leighton called to her, 'Either way, those young women will get justice. Maybe we should let you have your own *trial by water,* right? Give you same chance as they got, huh?'

After a moment of pointless resistance, Lina Brookes reluctantly reached for the orange rope, and gripped it. At the other end

Leighton and Troy slowly began to pull the woman from the wet sand. The effort of their task sent flashes of pain along Leighton's wounded foot but he figured it was less than the three victims would have endured, and so he was willing to tolerate it. In any case, Leighton knew he wouldn't need to hold on for long. Behind him a smattering of other officers was already hurrying along the beach to where he stood.

54

As he sat upright in an ambulance that was headed to Tri County Hospital, Leighton winced whilst a large make paramedic who was crouched in front of him wrapped a crepe bandage around his wounded foot.

'I think you might have got lucky here, buddy,' the paramedic said as he finished the task.

'You mean catching the murder suspect or getting shot in the foot?' Leighton asked as he tried to focus on keeping his throbbing foot still.

'I mean the fact the round isn't still in there, so the surgeon won't need to go digging around with a knife and spoon. Hopefully it'll just be a case of mend and send.'

'Thanks,' Leighton said, 'I guess it sounds luckier than it feels. Still hurts like hell.'

The paramedic sat up opposite Leighton and nodded.

'They'll give you a shot of something for the pain when you get up there. Unfortunately, we're not allowed to hit you up with any of the good stuff until you've been assessed.'

'So, after I've been seen and medicated, will I be free to go?'

'Sure. What's the hurry?  You could have a couple of days off duty with your foot on a cushion and the afternoon soaps on TV.'

'I have somebody I need to see.'

The paramedic glanced out of the rear window of the ambulance and smiled. 'Well, you'll be glad to know that we've arrived at County. Hopefully, they won't hold you too long.'

Thankfully, the paramedic had been accurate in his assessment of Leighton's injury. An x-ray confirmed that the 9mm slug has passed through outer side of his foot and exited in the underside.

However, he had been reliably informed that two small bones had been smashed by the gunshot and dealing with that required more than just a little first aid.

Leighton therefore was admitted and for emergency surgery. Just like many of the people he had arrested, he was permitted one phone call before being taken for treatment.

After injecting the site of the wound with anaesthetic, a trauma specialist, had cleaned the wound, dressed it with gauze and then bandaged the whole thing up again. Once, he was patched up, Leighton thanked the doctor then, before anyone could stop him he slid himself off the operating table. It was a mistake. As soon as he placed the injured foot tentatively on the floor, a flash of hot pain shot up his leg.

The doctor gave him another shot of morphine and, after explaining how he would have to walk very carefully, he gave him a pair of aluminium crutches and arranged for a large orderly to walk with him to limp to the accident and emergency reception.

'Is somebody coming to pick you up?' the orderly asked.

Leighton shook his head.

'You need to me call you cab then?'

'No thanks. I have somebody to see.'

'Here?'

'Yeah, she's up in high-dependency.'

The orderly looked at Leighton's crinkled, sand dusted clothes and his bandaged foot. 'Listen, I guess I can take you up there, but they might not let you through, until you've got yourself all cleaned up.'

'Can we try?' Leighton asked.

'Sure' the orderly smiled, and then led Leighton to the steel elevator doors.

As Leighton shifted uncomfortably on his crutches, the orderly pressed a button on a panel on the wall. There was a ping, and the doors slid open. Leighton felt a flicker of excitement in his stomach. However, at that moment, the doctor who had treated Leighton hurried into the reception area. He peered all around and then his face softened when he spotted Leighton. He strode over to him.

'Officer Jones, You're still here, good.'

'Why?'

'We got a message asking that you call the station.'

'Yeah, I'll do that from my apartment,'

'They said it was urgent,' the doctor said gravely. 'You can use one of the payphones on the wall behind you.'

Leighton looked at the elevator then to the phones.

'I'll wait for you,' the orderly said and gently patted Leighton on the shoulder.

Leighton limped over where four black payphones were mounted on the wall. He chose the nearest one and picked up the handset, slotted a coin in the slot and dialled the number.

'Hey, it's Leighton Jones,' he said, I' got a message to call.'

As he waited, the orderly stepped to one side to let a couple of nurses use the elevator. He then glanced back at the payphones and watched the wounded officer speak on the telephone for a moment, nodding as he listened intently. Then without warning, the officer let telephone handset drop from his hand and he slid down on to the white tiled floor and covered his face with his hands,

55

'Did you hear me?' the cab driver was twisted in his seat looking at Leighton who was clutching his crutches and staring at his knees.

'Huh?' Leighton looked up confused.

'I said, here we are, buddy.' The driver pointed to the Leighton's apartment building.

Leighton handed the driver a twenty, and then manoeuvred himself out of the vehicle. As the cab pulled away, Leighton stood in the dark street trying to compose himself for the arduous journey of climbing the stairs. He could feel the throb of pain emanating from his bandaged foot, however as he glanced up at his apartment window on the second floor, her forgot all about that. The light in the living room was on. That single rectangle of warm light meant only one thing – Heather was home.

It took Leighton almost ten minutes to ascend the two flights of stairs which led to the door of his apartment. One of the aluminium crutches he had been given at the hospital now lay at the bottom of the concrete stairs, where Leighton had thrown it after it served as more of a problem than an aid.

Eventually, he lowered himself down and sat on one of the steps. He then braced himself and began moving backwards up the stairs by using his placing his hands down on each edge and raising his butt one step at a time. As he moved slowly up each stair, Leighton kept his leg straight and the wounded foot raised off the ground. This method was quicker but keeping his leg in this position caused a painful cramp to descend over his knee and thigh on the side of the injury.

Finally, and dripping with sweat, Leighton reached the top landing.

He clambered to his feet, unlocked the door and let it swing open.

'Hey, Heather!' he called. 'You there?'

There was no answer.

Holding on to the wall, Leighton limped into the hall, and then closed the door. The place felt cold. He hobbled through to the living room, where a single lamp was on as if bravely holding back the darkness on its own. Leighton turned and hobbled to the bedroom where a single sheet of paper was lying on the bed. Leighton stumbled forwards and clumsily lowered himself to sit on the bed. It was a relief to have the weight finally off his foot. After pushing the redundant crutch away, he picked up the paper and read it.

> 'Leighton, I've had some time to think and it would seem best if we spent a few weeks apart. At least until I get my coursework completed. We can talk after that.

*I came back for some of my stuff today, but you were obviously out having fun. I'll pick up the rest later. H*

Leighton, let the paper fall from his hand and then stared at the blank wall of the bedroom. He had little emotional energy left to give.

But, in his mind he was watching a kaleidoscope of memories from what seemed like a thousand years earlier, he and Heather holding hands and kissing on the bleacher seating of Fontana high school, hiking through endless forests in the fall, wandering between the coloured stalls of the funfair in San Diego, painting their first apartment in their underwear, laughing and dreaming of a future filled with love and light.

Leighton wiped his eyes and then shifted his weight, swivelling his body trying to raise his legs up on to the bed. It was a painful manoeuvre, which suggested the second injection of morphine had almost worn off completely. A couple times the pain of movement was almost enough to make him give up, but eventually, Leighton managed it. However, once he had managed to complete the operation, Leighton looked down and noticed a dime-sized spot of blood was now seeping through the crepe bandage. He closed his eyes and ignored it. The effort of his ascent up the stairway had probably loosened some stitches and it was unlikely that he would bleed out. In any case, the damage to his foot was nothing in comparison to the emotional injury he had sustained.

Finally, Leighton sank into the dark waters of thoughtless sleep. It was something he welcomed.

## 55

The basement level of San Diego's formidable Metropolitan Correctional Centre featured a long windowless corridor lined with twenty-two steel doors. Each of the doors led to a cell for those prisoners who had newly arrived and were waiting induction and orientation, before eventually being transferred to the Pre-trial Unit. Despite the custard yellow walls, and external temperatures in the fifties, the basement area felt permanently cold and always smelled of industrial strength disinfectant.

At 5.25 p.m. two correctional officers dressed in light blue short-sleeved shirts and navy trousers were pushing a squeaking steel trolley along the corridor, and stopping at each door to hand out foil-wrapped trays of food. The two officers – Anna Tandy and Maria Murray-would often joke that this part of their job felt like delivering meals to each cell was like working as flight attendants on an endless trip. The two women had worked together for years and were a capable and efficient team.

'Hey, I meant to ask you on Monday but I forgot, how was your cousin's wedding?' Maria asked.

'Didn't I tell you? Lorenzo broke it off.'

'No way! You always said how happy the two of them looked together.'

'I know. He's an idiot. Always has been,' Anna said with a small shake of her head. 'My mom reckons he's been seeing someone he works with on the side.'

'Yeah?'

'Yep, my mom's usually right about these things. Apparently Carla has called my mom a couple of times looking for Enzo, after he had told her he was coming over to us for supper. It was bullshit of course.'

'What a rat!'

'If I was Carla I'd take a grinder to his truck.'

'Or some part of his anatomy,' Maria said with a laugh.

'Hey, talking of which, did you hear about our new arrival from Oceanside?' Anna asked

'No. What's the story with them?' Maria sounded genuinely disappointed. Usually she was one of the first members of staff to get the information on and new guests.

'Apparently it's some woman who found out her husband was cheating on her, so she murdered the three women he had been seeing.'

'Jeez!' Anna laughed. 'If my Ted ever started screwing around, I'd murder him and thank the poor bitch that had to put up with his baseball card collection and his beer gut.'

'Jealousy's a bitch,' Maria said as she slid another foil covered tray out of the insulated trolley.

When the two officers reached detention cell number twenty-three, Maria turned to Anna and nodded her head to one side, indicating that the prisoner they had been discussing was inside.

Maria gripped the worn handle of a steel hatch in the door and slid it open to reveal a long horizontal slot. She then pushed the meal on the aluminium tray through the hatch door to the room in which Lina was sitting.

'Come on Honey,' Maria called through the grille of the window, 'dinner time. Friday night is Tacos night!'

'I'm not hungry.' Lina said without moving from the narrow bed.

'Hey, just a couple of bites. You need to keep your strength up?'

For a moment Lina said nothing. Maria shrugged and pulled the tray back through the hatch.

'Well, I'm sure somebody else will want double.'

'I just have no appetite,' Lina said absently. 'I'm a grieving widow,' she added.

Maria frowned thoughtfully for a moment and peered through the opening at Lina. 'No honey you're just all mixed up,' she said in a sympathetic tone. 'I heard your husband was released this afternoon – so he's not dead at all.'

Lina glanced up at the clock on the wall shielded behind a wire cage. 'Well, perhaps not just yet...but he will be pretty soon,' she said quietly.

'Oh shit!' Maria said as she let the metal tray clatter to the floor, and then ran to find a telephone.

## 56

The grey coloured cab pulled up outside the Brooke's family home, its rear door opened and then Steve Brookes climbed out. He was in the same clothes as he been wearing when he was taken to the station six days earlier, but he looked a little less styled. There was no need to pay the driver whose services had been provided courtesy of Oceanside P.D. Brookes and his lawyer figured it would be the first of many compensatory payments he would receive from them.

As the car rumbled away, Brookes walked towards his house, swinging the clear plastic bag of personal belongings. Although he did not know it, Brookes was mirroring Leighton's earlier visit. However, this time there was only one car in the driveway.

When he reached the door of his property, Brookes discovered it was covered in criss-crossed yellow police tape like a strange spider's web. Frowning, Brookes pulled at it but the lurid material just stretched into thinner strands, which bit into the flesh of his hand. He traced the tape with his eyed and discovered that it was attached and realised it had been shut inside the door frame when the door had last been closed. He took out his keys from the bag, unlocked the door and pushed it open. The pieces of yellow tape fell from the frame like ticker tape as Brookes entered his home and then closed the door. Whilst his house was not particularly messy, it was clear that detectives had swept through the place whilst Brookes had been awaiting his release.

Crossing the hallway to the bedroom, Brookes smiled.

After the chaos of the last few weeks, he realised that he felt strangely liberated. Without Lina, he was now free to do whatever he wanted. His lawyer-Jim Stelling – had said that as long as Brookes refused to talk to prosecutors, he knew they would never be able to pin any responsibility on him. In any case, the lawyer was looking to secure immunity from prosecution in return for

Brookes giving evidence. He would simply present himself as another of Lina's victims and enjoy his liberty. It had even crossed his mind to one day write a book on his experience – cash-in on all the excitement.

Brookes had of course always suspected that Lina had done something to the girls. It was pretty obvious to him, after all, his wife had always had a jealous streak in her. He often recalled what happened when they had not been dating long and they had been out in a bar in Westmorland. After a few cocktails, Lina had gone to use the bathroom and Steve had begun to flirt with an attractive brunette waitress. When she returned, Lina had calmly ordered a flaming Sambuca, which she threw in the waitress' face. Fortunately, the flames had gone out upon impact and the woman waitress was more humiliated than hurt, but the chaos was enough to have them physically thrown out of the place. That same night, they had gone to bed and the sex was amazing, Lina was like a woman possessed — as if she was marking her territory or reminding Brookes what he had waiting at home.

Brookes had, inadvertently discovered the perfect way to push Lina's buttons. In the years that followed, he would often deliberately speak about attractive colleagues or students, knowing it would feed Lina's dark side.

Eventually, flirting with other women had simply become part of Brooke's everyday behaviour. But in the last six months it had grown to the point that it was no longer simply about making Lina jealous; it progressed on to sleeping with other people. Brookes was delighted to discover how receptive many vulnerable young women were to his advances. He, in turn, had become utterly intoxicated by them.

Despite his attempts to conceal the physical relationships he enjoyed with the girls, Lina had a way of sensing these things.

Perhaps in some primal way she could smell their scent lingering on him. But whatever the method, she knew, and whatever backseat frantic pleasure Brookes managed to get from any of the young women was suddenly stolen from him when they promptly disappeared.

Lina had never spoken about it, and he never found any evidence but Steve knew in his soul that she was involved in whatever happened to the girls.

This meant that with each new conquest, Brookes was aware that whichever young woman became his focus would later become his wife's focus too. But once they were gone, it simply became a matter of shifting the spotlight on to somebody new. If he was truly honest about it, the knowledge of how dangerous the affairs were for the women and for him, just added to his excitement.

As for Lina's current situation, Jim Daniels stated with some authority that it was highly unlikely that she'd be getting out of jail for at least twenty years – if at all.

Steve Brookes, it seemed had been set free in more ways than one. With Lina out of the way, he could indulge his pleasure without fear or conceal. Perhaps having his wife in locked up in jail would generate a degree of sympathy for Brookes, which would eagerly exploit.

After unbuttoning his shirt, he let it fall to the floor and gazed around at his new kingdom. The spacious bed would now be open to any female who took his fancy.

It was, he concluded, time to celebrate. He wandered through to the liquor cabinet and picked up a bottle of Scotch and a crystal glass. He poured a generous splash of amber liquid into the glass, then held it up in a private toast to his new found liberty.

'To Lina – one hell of a woman,' he said to the empty room. Then, in one smooth motion, Steve raised the ornate glass to his lips and threw back the entire contents.

After wincing against the spirit, Steve almost immediately uncorked the bottle again and began to fill the glass again.

It took a moment or two for Brookes to notice the strange sensation.

His usual bourbon would always have an initial fierce sting flooding his mouth and throat, but this was very different. The fire was all encompassing- scorching not just his mouth, but his entire insides. The glass bottle slipped from Brooke's hand, and landed on the floor where the contents continued to haemorrhage on to the carpet in regular glugs. The college lecturer realised what was happening and attempted to rush to the bathroom, hoping to vomit the liquid into the sculpted porcelain sink, but it was too late. His failing legs crumpled beneath him, and Brookes crashed on to the ground like a felled tree.

The fact that the bourbon concoction was approximately fifty percent rat poison, meant that his organs were already shutting down as he slammed on to the carpet.

As he lay face down on the bedroom floor, his mouth gulping his final futile breaths, Steve Brookes was vaguely aware that somewhere in the fading distance his telephone was ringing. He was however too far gone to hear by the time the answer-machine clicked on and a female voice spoke.

'Mr Brookes, this is Diane Wilson at the Metropolitan Correctional Facility. I need to speak to you urgently. You may be in danger. Please return this call as soon as you...'

The rest faded to silence.

# 57

Despite the warm evening, the waves were crashing against the legs of Oceanside Pier with all the intensity of a slowly gathering storm. At the far end of the structure the glass door of Rubies diner opened and Leighton Jones limped through the doorway. Walking was not quite as difficult for Leighton as it had been in the days immediately following the shooting, but it was still just as slow as he made his way to a small booth. Despite his doctor's stern advice, Leighton was no longer using the crutches, preferring instead to simply push through the pain.

The unpredictable weather meant that the diner was unusually quiet and the only other a couple of waitresses were leaning on the long counter chatting intently about some new Cher movie about witches.

Whilst Leighton eased himself carefully into a seat, one of the waitresses approached with a laminated cardboard menu.

'Hi, welcome to Rubies,' she said cheerfully. 'Would you like to see a menu?'

'No, it's fine.' Leighton said. 'Can just order?'

'Sure.' The waitress produced a small pad from her pocket. The gesture reminded Leighton of a cop. 'Okay, what would you like?'

'Two strawberry sundaes, please.'

'Two?'

'Yeah,' Leighton nodded.

'You feeling a little hungry?'

'No,' Leighton shifted a little in his seat. 'One of them is for a friend.

'Ah, you want me to hold of making them until your friend arrives?'

'No, thanks. You can just bring them right over.'

After the waitress had gone, Leighton dragged his hand over his face and the reached into his trouser pocket. He produced a small rattling bottle of pills and then unscrewed the lid.

It had been just over a week since Lina Brookes' had shot him in the foot, but the pain sometimes felt as fresh as if it had been the previous day. Things had however moved on... a little.

The worst part had been Alice's funeral service. After the cremation, he knew that everyone who was off duty would be heading over to The Rooster, eager to get drunk and move on from the morning's sombre mood. Leighton, however, was in no mood to party so decided to use the confusion of the departing crowd of mourners to slip away unseen.

However, as Leighton limped towards the waiting cab, he had heard someone call his name. Turning around he found Heather standing amongst the parked cars. Her eyes had looked lighter as she had walked over to Leighton and hugged him more tenderly than she had in many months.

'I'd like to come home,' she said softly.

Leighton held on to his wife as if she was a life preserver as they wept on each other's shoulders.

The following afternoon, the captain had asked Leighton if he wanted to clear out Alice's locker. The captain had said that he was willing to do it, but that he felt Leighton was probably the closest thing to family Alice had. Leighton didn't want to delve into Alice's privacy, but more importantly he didn't want anyone else doing that either. He knew that information could spread round a police station faster than wildfire, and he didn't want anything from Alice's locker becoming public knowledge.

I t contained very little other than a spare white t shirt, a bicycle puncture repair kit and small white bag of toiletries. There was also a pair of sunglasses in a clamshell case. However, on the inside of the door, a polaroid photograph of had been taped to the grey metal. As Leighton peeled the picture from the door, he realised what it was. It seemed like the photograph was from another lifetime rather than just a week earlier.

Tonight, as Leighton sat in the empty diner with two melting ice-cream sundaes before him- the strawberry sauce running down the sides as if on like lava on snow covered volcanoes- he reached into his jacket pocket and pulled out the photograph his friend had taken. He held up the Polaroid picture and looked at it.

The officer leaning against the cruiser looked younger and more carefree than the man Leighton had become in recent days. But he was less concerned with that than he was with the officer who had taken the photograph. Traffic Officer Alice Mead – had been six days from retirement after serving the community for thirty-two years when she had essentially been killed on one of the roads she had patrolled every week.

'Happy retirement, Alice,' Leighton had said quietly. 'We did it.'

Then turned the photo over to read, Alice's scrawled writing on the back.

*Rookie Jones, best partner I ever had.*

Leighton offered a sad smile, and then carefully placed the photo on the table. If Alice had considered him the best Rookie, then he would carry that torch for her and aim to be the best damned cop he could be. Not the highest ranking. She wouldn't have cared for that. He would just try to help people and that, at least, seemed good enough.

On the shore opposite the pier, the tall palm trees swayed like drunk giants and beyond that the city of Oceanside prepared for the gathering storm...

## 58

Lina Brookes was making her prison bed, when a shadow passed over the wall opposite her. Turning around, she found herself looking at a large woman with sunken eyes. She was dressed in standard issue orange overalls and standing in the doorway, as large and as immovable as a stone memorial.

'Your name Brookes?' the large woman grunted.

'What if I am- who the hell are you?' Lina said as she stood up folding her arms across her chest.

The large woman nodded. 'I just wanted to stop by and welcome you. Name's Maggie – Maggie Levin. I think you knew my baby girl – Sarah.'

Before Lina Brookes had time to register the name, the woman moved incredibly quickly for her size. In a single move, she lunged into the cell simultaneously pulling the home-made blade-

fashioned from a sharpened piece of a smashed toilet lid- from inside her sleeve.

Lina Brookes lunged to one side but was not fast enough to avoid the attack, which involved the large woman grabbing her chin and then delivering three sudden squelching stabs into the side of her throat.

Within six seconds of entering the jail cell, Maggie Levin left quite casually. Behind her, Lina Brookes lay gasping like a beached fish, face down in a widening pool of hot blood soaking into her freshly made bed.

Epilogue

Almost six weeks had passed since Leighton heard of Lina's Brookes murder in the women's penitentiary. The crime had probably meant that Maggie Levin – who had been eligible for parole the following April, would now never be released. But

Leighton figured that the woman, who had no spouse and had lost her only child, had little to want to leave for. At least prison gave her a family of sorts.

The sun was hotter than usual for the start of February, as Leighton pulled his Duster off the grey tarmac of Grapefruit Road a couple of miles to the east of Salton Sea. The surrounding area – true to the road name – was filled with endless rows of citrus fruit groves. Leighton liked how it gave the landscape a neat and orderly appearance, yet was still bursting with life. He slowed the car to a stop outside a small bone coloured house. As he climbed out of the car, Leighton glanced at the flimsy wire fence which secured the boundary of the dead garden. He pushed open the small gate and then walked up the cracked path set like stepping stones in a sea of parched earth. A red plastic crate overflowing with empty tequila bottles sat to the side of the front door. Leighton glanced up at the shuttered windows, but the dark slits gave nothing away. He reached out and pressed the sun-baked buzzer, and wasn't surprised to hear no sound, so he then made a fist and banged on the frame of the screen door. It felt like the thing might fall apart.

Eventually, a scrawny man wearing colourless pants and a stained white vest appeared in the opposite side of the screen.

'Ray Brander?'

'I am. What's it to you?' he rasped.

'My name is Leighton Jones?'

'Come again.'

Leighton pulled out his badge and held it up to the screen.

'Leighton Jones – from Oceanside PD. We spoke on the telephone back in October.'

'Oh, yeah. You were asking about missing persons. So, did you get a conviction for the guy.'

'Yes we did, but my hunch was only half right.'

'How d' you mean?'

'Turned out it was the suspect's wife who was the killer.'

'Yeah, woman can surprise you.' Brander said with a dry chuckle. 'So what you doing up here?'

'You remember the name you gave me- Ellie Johnstone from the trailer park at Redhill Marina?'

'Sure – she's a missing person. If your lady killer was up here around that time, they could easily have taken her too. Impossible to know who did it for sure unless a body shows up.'

'Or they confess,' Leighton suggested.

'Sure,' Brander shrugged, 'or they confess.'

'Well here's the thing- during the pre-trial, the prosecution team couldn't find anything linking the suspect or her husband to Ellie Johnstone.'

'Well, it was just a theory. I never promised you it was anything other than that. Now, if you don't mind, I've got supper to fix.' Brander said and began to turn away.

'I have a theory too Mr Brander,' Leighton said softly.

Brander stopped mid turn and looked at Leighton.

'What the fuck you talking about?'

'You see when I realised that Brookes had nothing to do with Ellie Johnstone, I did a little digging. Turns out that her boss from The Red Lantern Inn – Shannon Delroy- doesn't work there anymore.'

'No fucking wonder, it was almost six years ago. People move on. Maybe you should too.'

'But I managed to track her down all the same. She lives over in Glamis now – working in a motel just off Highway 78.'

'So?'

'Turns out she remembers Ellie pretty clearly. Says she was a good worker, despite occasional visits from her loudmouth boyfriend– Dwayne Barclay- looking for cash. Ms Delroy said the guy would always leave her rattled.'

'I told you Barclay was an asshole. If your lady killer didn't do it, my second choice would be that guy.'

Leighton nodded and then continued. 'Ms Delroy also said that Ellie had a thing going with an older married man- possibly a cop, who drove down to the bar every night and gave her a ride home. Ellie talked about the guy as if he knew about the law and stuff and could get her away from here. The guy never came into the bar, just always waited at the far end of the parking lot in what Ms Delroy referred to as a 'rust coloured Buick'. Apparently, during the last shift Ellie worked, she was really upset, kept bursting into tears all night. She had found out she was pregnant and it couldn't be Dwayne's as he was doing a six week stretch in Calipatria. But on that last night, the older guy didn't show up to give her a ride home. That's why Ellie was driving the old Dodge. Ms Delroy figured that the older guy had broken up with her over the pregnancy.'

'You're wasting my fucking time here,' Brander said, turned for second time and began walking away.'

'She also told me that she gave all of this information to the cop who was in charge of the investigation,' Leighton called loudly. 'That was you- Detective Raymond H Brander!' Only the thing is – none of that information was ever entered into the case notes. That got me wondering why you didn't tell me any of that either when we spoke on the phone, so I checked and according to DMV records he drove a 1980 Buick Skylark in Cinnabar – most folks just called it rust-coloured. So you wanna hear my theory – before I take it to your old boss?'

Brander suddenly turned back and lurched towards the screen door, his face contorted in rage. 'What's the fucking theory, Einstein – that I knocked up some little trailer-park piece of ass then got rid of her? Why the hell would I do that?'

'Probably to save your marriage, stop you getting fired, and keep Dwayne Barclay from punching the shit out of you?'

'Well, any sane person would've done the same thing, And I'll tell you something else – if that little slut had been on the pill like she fuckin' claimed, she would still be alive today.'

'If you didn't want to be with her you could have just helped her to get away – start a new life – like you promised.'

'Yeah right, and pay for two families for the rest of my goddamned life. You should know how shit law enforcement get paid. She would've bled me dry.'

'You will face justice,' Leighton said firmly.

'Well, without a body and no physical evidence, it's gonna be your word versus mine – you think anyone could build a case around that?'

Leighton said nothing.

'You see,' Brander nodded assertively, 'that's why dumb fuck traffic cops like you are better off staying the hell away from Homicide. You're out of your depth and sinking fast.'

'Yeah, I guess that could be true.' Leighton said thoughtfully. It was his turn to walk away from the screen door. 'Unless, of course, the *dumb fuck traffic cop* had already visited this area two weeks ago and presented all of this information to Chief Arnold at Westmorland station, who put together a successful affidavit requesting authorisation of a wire to record our conversation today.'

Ray Brander's eruption in a flow hateful insults were drowned out by the sudden banshee sound of three police cruisers, which screeched to a halt alongside Leighton's car. As a number of local officers ran by him to smash their way into Ray Brander's home and wrestle the writhing man into submission, Leighton Jones walked calmly away from the house. He pushed through the small gate, and then moved to his car and leaned on the hood. The sweet aroma of the surrounding Oranges and Apricot groves filled the air. Leighton breathed in the fragrant aroma as he felt the warmth of the sun on his face. He felt that, for the first time in months, he was finally emerging from the darkness, which had engulfed him – and the light felt good.

***

Printed in Great Britain
by Amazon